A Lady and

A Boss

Written By: Mz.

Lady P

D1521437

Text Shan to 22828 to stay up to date with new releases, sneak peeks, contest, and more...

Check your spam if you don't receive an email thanking you for signing up.

Text SPROMANCE to 22828 to stay up to date on new releases, plus get information on contest, sneak peeks, and more!

Previously In Heart of Stone

I had just been escorted back to my cell after being sentenced to ten years in prison. That would be served at the Dixon Correctional Center in Dixon, IL. When my sentence was read, I looked behind me and saw Kartier holding Shannie as she cried. I became saddened as Boss got up and exited the courtroom.

As for me, I held my head high and accepted my punishment. I was now twelve weeks pregnant, and I was barely showing, which was a good thing. At this point, I knew that I wasn't going to get an abortion. This baby had to be a gift from God. He wouldn't bless me with another child if it wasn't in his plans.

I was able to get one last visit before I was shipped off to serve my prison sentence. I already knew that I wanted Shannie to come. She hadn't been able to come and visit, but when I called and told her we needed to talk, she agreed to come.

*****

"Hey, Shannie, you look like you're about to pop."

"I wish. I'm only six months and this baby is huge. That's enough about me, K'Yonnah. How are you holding up?"

"I'm good, considering my condition. As far as going to prison goes, I'm ready to get that shit over with."

"Condition? What do you mean by that?"

"I'm three months pregnant," I said through tears.

"Oh my God, Yonnah! I'm sorry, but it's just like Stone's ass to fuck your life up after death. I can't believe this shit."

"I'm in shock too, but there's something else I have to tell you."

"What?"

"I'm not pregnant by Stone. This is Boss' baby. That's why I called you down here. It's too late for me to get an abortion and the last thing I want to do is give birth and give my baby to a stranger. I was wondering if you and Kartier could get the baby for me when I have it. I know that Boss has to know I'm pregnant with his child, but can you tell him after the baby is born. I don't want him worrying about me while I'm in here pregnant. I've caused him enough headaches. Please, do this for me. I have a bank account with a nice amount of money. I'm going to give you all of the information that you need to have access to the funds."

"You have to know that Boss will want his child. We can't keep something like this from him. I know you mean well, K'Yonnah, but he has to know. Without a doubt, you know that Boss will take care of that baby. Not only that, Kartier and I will make sure our godchild wants for nothing. Please don't cry, K'Yonnah. We're your family and we will be here every step of the way, and when you're done with your sentence, God willing, we'll all be there with open arms, waiting to receive you. I love you so much."

"I love you too. Please make sure my baby knows that I'm sorry I couldn't be there for him. Tell Boss I never meant for any of this to happen, and I'm sorry. I'll be in touch." I blew her a kiss and got ready to go and start my prison sentence.

As I rode the bus to prison, I couldn't help but think about how things would have turned out had I told the authorities about the abuse that I was enduring at the hands of Stone. I really don't even understand how I stayed for so long and allowed him to treat me like shit when I knew that I deserved so much more out of life.

In my opinion, one of the biggest misconceptions about domestic violence is that it's just physical. Pain doesn't only come from your significant other's fist. It's the pain they put on your mind. Stone mentally abused me and that's worse than any punch, kick, or slap he could ever give me. Wounds and scars heal in time; mental abuse stays with you forever.

Stone brought me up, to bring me down every chance he got. Stone mind fucked me something terrible. To lay up with a man who saw you go through so much pain, knowing he inflicted it on you is enough to drive any woman crazy.

How will I ever be the same in life, knowing my parents and my daughter died at the hands of a man who claimed to love me? What's worse is that there was a time when I loved him more than anything in this world. I could go on and on about what he did to me, but then I would be playing the victim. In reality, I was a victim, but I should have said something.

If I had, I wouldn't have been convicted of killing the sorry son of a bitch. I suffered in silence for a long time before I even told Shannie what was going on in my home. I gave Stone power over me. He knew I feared him, and he used that to his advantage. He had me thinking that all I had in this life was him. I wish I would have loved myself just a little bit more. I would have seen all the signs and took heed to them.

Stone was a snake the moment he approached me, knowing full well he killed my parents. If I could give advice to any woman in the world who is in a domestic violence relationship, it would be to get out while you can. The first time a man feels the need to put his hands on you, you should leave.

Ain't no such thing as "baby, I'm sorry" or "I'll never hit you again". Truth is, if they did it once, they'll do it again. If you forgive him, you're opening the floodgates to something much more than you could have ever bargained for.

Most importantly, make sure you report it to the proper authorities. The best thing a woman could ever do is keep a paper trail when she's in that type of situation. It will definitely work out in her favor. Lord knows I wish I had done all of those things and more. I can't sit and focus on the "what ifs" or feel sorry for myself because then it would be like I have regrets about killing him. I will never regret killing Stone. The only thing I will ever regret is not protecting my daughter from her father.

Fast Forward- 2015

After only serving five years of my ten-year prison sentence, I was released, and placed on home monitoring. A lot had changed in the five years that I had been away. I took courses to become a domestic violence counselor. I talked to other prisoners about domestic violence awareness.

I had a calling and I knew what I wanted to do once I got out. I had every intention of opening up a domestic violence shelter for battered women. While I was away, Shannie and Boss made sure to look after the property that Stone had taken from my father. What better way than to give it back to my cause by turning it into a place to help battered women.

Boss kept me up-to-date on our son's life. He's now four, going on five, and is the spitting image of his father. Throughout my sentence, we have remained the best of friends. I'll be the first to admit, I was kind of hurt when I found out he was getting married to his girlfriend, Meesha, but I knew our ship had sailed.

Plus, she had been there for my son; he called her mom. I was grateful for her and Boss taking care of him. He knew I was his real mother, and that's what mattered most to me. Boss kept his promise and had been there my whole sentence. I was now out and living with Kartier and Shannie until I got off of electronic monitoring. I couldn't wait to start my new life. I wanted nothing more than to raise my son and open up my domestic violence shelter. There's so much more to come in the life of K'Yonnah Kyles.

Introducing A Lady and A Boss

Chapter 1- K'Yonnah

I had been sitting outside of Boss and Meesh's home, contemplating going inside. The exterior was absolutely beautiful. I could only imagine what the inside looked like. A part of me wanted to drive away because I felt so inadequate. I'm still living with Shannie and Kartier until my house is finished. They make me feel so comfortable, but I feel like I'm in their way. They have two kids now and are living an amazing life. Since I'm off of house arrest, I've been looking high and low for an apartment. Shannie is going to be so mad at me for not telling her that I'm moving out. I just need to be more independent for my son. He's living in the lap of luxury with his father and I just want him to have his own space at my place.

I sat nervously smoking a cigarette. I picked up the bad ass habit when I was in jail and it's hard as hell to stop. Whenever I'm feeling nervous or anxious, I smoke one, and that's the majority of the time. Since my release, I'm learning to adapt to being a free woman. The shit is so hard, but I'm a strong ass woman and I will be okay. I had been avoiding Boss at all costs because I was so afraid to look at him. We had kept in touch over the years via phone calls here and there. He would also send pictures of our son, along with drawings. I never received any letters from him, but Shannie made sure to keep me informed. I went into a deep depression when I learned about Boss and Meesh getting married. It took me a month to get my mind right after that. So here I am, getting ready to have dinner with the man I was madly in love with and his wife. This shit feels so awkward, but at the same time, I want to spend some time with my son. After

I sprayed on some perfume a

my mouth. It was time for

panties on and face the pe

while I was away. I know th...

a new life, but this shit feels like a death sentence

because I know my heart is going to break seeing

Boss and Meesh together.

******

"I'm so glad you agreed to come and have

dinner with us. The boys should be here any minute."

Meesh was walking around in Red Bottoms and a

beautiful lounging gown. She was so beautiful. Her

hair was cut short in one of those pixie cuts and it

complemented her small, round face. Her light skin

tone looked so flawless. Not to mention she was

thicker than a Snicker. I could see why Boss wifed

her. I give the bitch credit; she was bad in every

sense of the word. At the same time, I couldn't help

but feel like she was flaunting their lifestyle in my

Not to mention all the fucking ice she was cking. Like really, who cooks dinner dressed like that.

"Thank you for inviting me. I can't tell you how much it means to me that you took care of my son while I was away. I really appreciate it, Meesh."

"Oh, no problem. I love my baby. With his spoiled butt." As soon as the words left her mouth, Boss and our son walked into the living room where we were sitting.

"Hey, Mommy! Look what I got." My son ran full speed ahead past me and into the arms of Meesh. My heart broke into a million pieces. I just wanted to leave at that moment. I held my composure though because there was no reason for me to be upset. After all, she is technically the only mother he's known.

"Wow! That's a nice airplane," Meesh said as she wrapped her arms around him. I turned around and locked eyes with Boss. He was still sexy as hell. His dark chocolate skin was glowing and his dreads were braided into a neat fishtail. The wife beater and gray jogging pants looked so fucking good on his body. His abs were on point and the bulge in his pants was giving me flashbacks of the first time he made love to me. I became entranced just looking at him. Boss walked towards me and pulled me into his embrace.

"Welcome home, Yonnie. It's good to have you home."

"Thanks, Boss. It's great to be home." I wiped the tears from my eyes that had fallen. Being in Boss' arms was the best feeling ever. At the same time, I knew just from his touch alone I was still in love with him. It had been so long since I've physically felt the touch of a man's hand, so his touch had me seeing fireworks.

"Let's eat before it gets cold," Meesh said, which caused us to break our embrace. We had both forgotten she was in the room. I looked at her and I could see the jealousy in her face.

"Give us a minute alone with Lil Boss."

"Really, Karion?"

"Fuck you mean really. Yes, we need to have a minute with our son. It's no disrespect to you, Meesh, but they need this time to get acquainted. As a matter of fact, we're going to go out for dinner so they can bond. It's kind of hard doing that with you being right here. It will make him all nervous."

"Can I come too? I mean, I have raised him as my own. He's my son too, Karion."

"That's true, you did raise him, but she birthed him. The answer to your question is no. I'll see you when I get back." Boss grabbed our son's hand and they walked out of the door with me in tow. I looked back and I could see the hurt on Meesh's face. I felt like I needed to say something to her.

"I appreciate you for raising my son, Meesh, but the fact remains the same; I birthed him, not you. I didn't come here to cause any trouble; I just want to build a relationship with my son."

"You just remember that I'm Mrs. Karion "Boss" Miller," she said as she slammed the door in my face. There were so many things I could have said to her but now was not the time. One thing for sure and two for certain, that would be the last time the bitch disrespects me.

*****

It felt so funny sitting across from Boss and our son; they were the spitting image of one another. Thinking back to the first time I ever laid eyes on him, I never imagined in a million years he would be the father of my child. I became sad as my mind drifted to my daughter Kierra; she would be six years old now. Thinking of her made me think about Stone and I had to hurry up and shake the thought of him from my mind. I was sitting across from my son and that's all I needed to focus on. We were at The Cheesecake Factory, eating dessert and getting better acquainted with one another.

"Do you have to go back to jail, K'Yonnah?" Karion Jr. asked out of the blue.

"No, baby, I never have to go back to that place and I'm so sorry I had to go there in the first place. Mommy promises that she will never leave you again." I got up and pulled him in for a hug.

"I can't call you Mommy, K'Yonnah." I was taken aback by hearing him say that.

"You want me to beat your ass, lil nigga? That's how you address her. I never want to hear you call her K'Yonnah again." Karion started to cry and that's the last thing I wanted to see him do. I could tell he didn't play with Boss at all.

"It's okay, Boss. He has to get used to having me around."

"No, it's not okay, Yonnah. Stop him from doing that shit now before it gets out of hand. I hate to hear a child call their mother by their first name. That shit is so fucking disrespectful. He doesn't call Meesh by her name and he for damn sure ain't about to address you by yours." It warmed my heart to see Boss instilling respect in our son, but in a way, I think he was being a little hard on him.

"I'm sorry, Daddy, but it's not my fault. Mommy told me to call her K'Yonnah." Karion buried his face into his father's chest. Boss and I locked eyes and I could see the anger in his and I'm quite sure he could see the pain in mine. It took everything inside of me not to go the fuck off. Here I am trying to give this bitch all the praise for being here for my son. Before today, I held the hoe in high regard, but this bitch was a snake. I couldn't believe she was trying to turn my son against me. I couldn't wait to tell Shannie about this shit. I reached across the table and pulled him around to the side of the booth that I was sitting on.

"Come over here, Karion. Let me tell you something that I think you should know. You're a big boy, so I'm going to always treat you as such. Mommy hurt someone really bad and the police sent me to jail because you can't hurt people, no matter what they do to you. I love you baby and I promise that I will never leave you again. Do you forgive me, Karion?"

"Yes, Mommy, I forgive you." I grabbed my baby so tight and hugged him with everything inside of me. The tears were flowing and I damn near broke down when my baby started to wipe my tears. Boss got up and pulled me up from the seat and wrapped his arms around me.

"Stop crying, ma. You're home now and that's all that matters. In the past, all I saw was you crying. I want to see you smile going forward. I know that I'm married to Meesh, but I'll be here for you no matter what."

It felt so good to hear him speak those words, but it felt even better to be in his arms. His Armani Code cologne was so damn intoxicating. I needed to get away from this man; I had no business having these nasty thoughts I was having knowing he was married.

Chapter 2- Boss

Seeing K'Yonnah after all these years brought back memories of wanting to be with her. I had long ago put our brief encounter in the back of my mind. That was the easy part of her being away. The hard part was looking at my son every day and being reminded that his mother was in jail. Not to mention the fact that he had her eyes. Those beautiful eyes. He was going to have the women on his ass. After all, he looks like his father so he's definitely going to get mad pussy.

I was glad K'Yonnah and our son had a chance to bond. They needed that time alone. Just knowing that Meesh would tell my son to be disrespectful to K'Yonnah had me feeling some type of way. I was actually glad that Lil Boss had gone to sleep. I didn't want him to hear me curse Meesh the fuck out. Her telling him to call K'Yonnah by her name was way out of line and real fucked up on her part.

When I walked inside of the bedroom, Meesh was sitting up in bed, watching TV. I removed my shoes and sat down on the edge of the bed. I needed to calm down before I spazzed out on her ass. As soon as I walked in the room, she rolled her eyes so hard I thought those shits were going to get stuck like that. I grabbed the remote and turned the TV off. I needed her undivided attention.

"I was watching that."

"I need to holla at you for a minute on some real shit."

"About what?" she said with an attitude and she rolled her eyes again like I was getting on her nerves or something.

"I'm going to need you to fix your motherfucking face. You're the last person that should be sitting up with a fucking attitude. What's this shit I hear about you telling Lil Boss not to call K'Yonnah momma?" I flamed up a blunt, waiting for her ass to say something. The stupid ass look on her face let me know that she was guilty as fuck. Not that I didn't believe my son, but the last thing a nigga wanted was for his wife to be devious. I don't like this shit one bit because I would have never allowed her to step in and co-parent with me. From the jump, she's always been good to Lil Boss. He loves her, so there was no reason for her to say that shit to him.

"I'm sorry, Karion. I know that it was wrong. I just felt that with her being home, everything was going to change for us. He's not going to need me anymore. Not to mention, I saw the way she was looking at you earlier. She wants you and Lil Boss. You know that all I have in this world is y'all. Promise me that you won't leave me." Meesh was crying and that made me move over closer to her.

"Come on now, bae. What you crying for? I'm not about to leave you. K'Yonnah and I are Lil Boss' parents, so that's something that you have to deal with. Just because she's home doesn't take away the fact that you have been here for him since day one. K'Yonnah knows that you love Lil Boss as if he was your own. She appreciates the fact that you stepped in and helped me take care of him. At the same time, you can't be telling him shit like don't call her momma. That makes her look at you sideways. When I heard him say it, I couldn't believe that you said some shit like that. You're my wife and I love you Meesh, but don't you ever in your life tell my son no bullshit like that. You have no reason to feel insecure because K'Yonnah is home. There is nothing between us." I reached over and wiped the tears that had fallen. I love my wife and the last thing I want her to do is feel inadequate because Yonnah is out of prison. Meesh has been my rider and that's why I put a ring on it.

"Can we try for our baby now?"

"You know that's not a good idea. The last time you had a miscarriage, it was rough on you. It's just too soon and I'm not ready for you to go through that again. Plus, the doctor said it's not good on your body. Let's just give it another six months." Meesh knows full well it's too soon for us to try and get pregnant again. She's been pregnant twice, and both times she's had miscarriages at the four-month mark. That shit has been hard on a nigga. Not to mention dealing with her bouts of depression following the miscarriages. Meesh shouldn't even want to go through that again. I know that she's only trying to do it because K'Yonnah is out. I kissed her on the forehead and I left out of the room before she had a chance to say anything. This shit was not up for discussion. I went and sat in my office and laid my head back in my chair. I closed my eyes and all I could see was K'Yonnah. Jail had done her body good as fuck. I adjusted my dick picturing her fat ass. The sound of Meesha clearing her throat made me jump from lusting over K'Yonnah.

"Are you coming to bed or not?"

"Yeah, I'm on my way, bae." I jumped up and she grabbed my hand, leading me to our bedroom.

She started to undress and at the same time, my phone started to ring. I answered and it was K'Yonnah telling me that her car had stopped and she needed me to call someone to help her.

"That was K'Yonnah. Her car stopped and she needs me to help her." Meesha placed her clothes back on and climbed in bed. I could tell she wanted to say something.

"What?" I asked.

"Nothing. Cut the light off on your way out." She pulled the covers over her and turned her back to me. I had never seen her act this jealous in my life. I hated she felt that way. At the same time, I was not about to leave K'Yonnah stranded to spare Meesh's feelings. Her feelings were going to be hurt a lot more because I was not going to mistreat my baby momma to make her ass happy.

*****

When I pulled up behind K'Yonnah's car, she was sitting inside on the phone. When she saw me, she hung up and got out of the car. I got out of my car as well and walked towards her.

"I'm so sorry that I had to bother you, Karion. I just had my car serviced. I don't know what's wrong with it."

"It's cool. Pop the hood so I can see what's going on." I rolled up my sleeves and lifted the hood. I looked around and realized that she had some wires loose and that's why it stopped on her. I hooked them back up and closed the hood.

"You're all good now, Yonnie. It was just some loose wires. I hooked them back up. You should be all good now."

"I'm so glad that's all it was. Thanks again for coming out when I called." K'Yonnah looked like she was nervous as hell to be around me. The closer I walked to her, the faster she walked towards the driver's side of the car. I felt the need to at least reassure her that anything she needs, I'm here for her. I hated that she was different than before she got locked up. Of course, prison changes people, but I hate that for her. The more I stared at her, the more I became attracted to her. She got inside her car and I closed the door behind her.

"Look, don't feel like you're a burden when it comes down to the things you need. I know you really don't have family, but I'm your family. Let me know if there's anything you need, Yonnie. Don't be afraid to ask, okay?" I watched as she held her head down and twiddled her fingers nervously. I lifted her chin and made her look at me in my eyes. One thing led to another and I kissed her. Surprisingly, she opened her mouth and allowed me to slip her the tongue. It brought back that familiar feeling between us. As soon as I got all the way into it, she pushed me back.

"No, Karion! We can't. I'm sorry about that. I have to go." She drove off so fast I had to jump back to keep her from rolling over my feet. I was so mad at myself for kissing her. Then again, a nigga couldn't help it. Her pink lips looked so juicy. I couldn't help but do it. I just stood there looking at her car disappear from my sight. A text notification chimed and I already knew it was Meesh. I looked at the screen and she was asking where I was. I didn't even respond; I just headed straight to the crib and took a cold ass shower. I had a hard on out of this world for my baby momma. If Meesh even had an inkling, she was going to go crazy.

Chapter 3-K'Yonnah

My mind was going into overdrive trying to wrap my mind around what had just happened between Karion and I. For so long while I was in prison, I yearned for him sexually. His lips were still so soft. When he broke the news that he was getting married, I put him in the back of my mind. This kiss had done nothing but add to my desire for him. However, I know that what we had is over. He's now a married man and the last thing I want to do is ruin his marriage.

I know he must think I'm crazy as hell for driving off like that, but I had to get the hell out of there. That kiss took me back to when I realized that I loved Boss. At the same time, I was in the process of trying to get over the death of my daughter and away from Stone with his psycho ass. I taught myself a long time ago to suppress memories that had the ability to hurt my growth. Boss was a good memory, but I feel like if I put him in the back of my mind, it won't hurt seeing him with his wife. I just wish I could turn back the hands of time and allow Boss to love me. By the time I realized he was all that I needed, it was too late. I had killed Stone, was convicted of his murder, and was pregnant with Lil Boss. I don't regret anything, though. The greatest thing to come out of all of this is my son. I only wish that I could have been out in the world to raise him. I know that he loves me, but I feel like he doesn't know me. I plan on changing that real soon. Hopefully, Boss and Meesh allow me to be a full-time parent instead of him spending the night with me. There shouldn't be a problem because he was only supposed to be with them temporarily. However, I don't want to take him from all that he knows. I just want my baby home with me so I can be the mother that I'm supposed to be. In reality, he's all that I have in this world. I have no blood relatives that are living.

*****

"Are you okay, K'Yonnah? All day your mind has been somewhere else. I feel like I've been talking to myself all day," Shannie said as she filed away intake papers.

"I'm sorry, friend. What were you saying?"

"Spill the beans. What's going on?" I was dreading this. That's why I had really been avoiding conversation. I didn't want anyone to know about the kiss that Boss and I shared. Shannie is my best friend in the whole wide world so it's only right that I tell her. I just don't want her being all dramatic. Somewhere in her mind, she feels like Boss and I are going to be married and live happily ever after.

"Boss kissed me last night."

"Yasss bitchhhh yassss!"

"Nooooo bitchhh noooo! That shit should not have happened. Boss is married and I'm not trying to fuck up that man's marriage. Not to mention the fact that his wife raised my son. I'm not one of those women who come in and break up happy homes."

"K'Yonnah, please. Let me tell you something about happy homes. That's how that shit looks on the outside. Those homes have leaky roofs, runny faucets, and cracks in the foundation. If a couple's home is as happy as they portray it to be, it wouldn't be easy for anyone to just slide in and break it up. Trust and believe me, Boss and Meesh's home is about to crumble." I looked at Shannie crazy, but at the same time, dying to know more.

"Why do you say that?"

"You, of course."

"Don't say that, Shannie. I'm not trying to come in between that man and his wife. I just want to co-parent and be cordial for the sake of our son."

"I know that it's not your intention to break up their home. One thing for sure and two for certain, Boss is very much still in love with you. Meesh was something to do when there was nothing to do. Now don't get me wrong, I strongly believe that he loves her. Hell, I'll even go as far as to say that he's in love with her. However, the fact remains the same that he loves you and what you two have has been special from the jump. Boss has always been in love with you, K'Yonnah. You went away and he had to continue on with life. That nigga talked about you all day every day. At one point, he was talking about hiring lawyers and paying whatever he could to get you out of prison. That man might be married, but you got his heart.

Not to mention God gave you and him the greatest gift in the form of another life. You have something that Meesh can't give him and that's a baby. Every time she gets pregnant, she has a miscarriage. When that happens, she goes into a deep ass depression. I think the bitch crazy for real, but that's just my opinion. At any rate, I just want you to stop walking around here like you being in jail was this big bad thing that ruined your life. Meesh raised him, yes, but fuck her. She's not his mother. We both know she only took him in because he was a part of the package. Meesh has never done anything to me, but I hate that she tries to act like she is his biological mother. You're home now and it's time for her to step aside and let you do what you have to do." Before I could respond, the door opened and in walked Meesh.

"Speak of the Devil," I muttered under my breath so that Shannie could hear me.

"This bitch be dressing like she in Paris on a runway." I tried my best not to laugh. Meesh was doing the most, though. She was rocking a long flowing dress that swept the floor as she walked, draped in diamonds, huge designer shades, and a long weave. I admit she looked good, but who was she trying to impress. I really felt like she was trying to throw her wealth in my face. I had money as well, but I didn't have to walk around flaunting it.

"Can we talk, K'Yonnah?" she said with an attitude.

"Of course. Step into my office."

"You guys can stay here and talk. I need to go do inventory in the rooms for the ladies we have coming in later," Shannie said as she got up and headed towards the residences that had been added on to my domestic violence center. We had gotten our first two occupants and I were overly excited to help the women who also had children. I thanked God for Kierra's Place. My daughter's spirit was all over this place. She was indeed my guardian angel.

"So what brings you by here?" I asked.

"I'm going to get straight to the point because I don't have time for bullshit. I know that you want Boss. That stunt you pulled last night was classic. I have to give it to you. I underestimated you. You're not like the other bitches he cheats with. He treats you special and that's an issue for me. I'm the only special woman in his life. You see this rock on my finger; I worked hard for it. As a matter of fact, I would kill for it. I've worked hard to solidify my place as Mrs. Karion Miller. I haven't come this far to lose to a felon. Last night when my husband came home, he had pink lipstick all over his lips. The same cheap pink lipstick you have on now. I know you have ulterior motives and that Goody Two-shoe behavior you exhibit is a façade. I know that you want my life, but as long as I breathe air I'll never let you have it easily." I was trying my best not to take it there with this bitch, but the more she talked, the more I realized she thought she was fucking with a punk or something. This was this bitch's last time coming for me. It was one thing for her to disrespect me at her house, but my place of business was the ultimate no-no. If I let this bitch keep sliding, she will start thinking she can skate. I didn't want to take it there with the bitch, but I had to hurt her feelings real quick.

"This is the second time you called yourself handling me. There will not be a third. Let's get some shit straight, Meesh. Boss might be your husband, but it's me he lusts for when he's fucking you. Get you some business, bitch, before I really hurt your feelings. That nigga is the father of my son, nothing more and nothing less. Trust and believe me if I wanted him, I could have him. K'Yonnah will always and forever be all over his lips like liquor. You just sit back and think about which lips I'm talking about. I'm glad I know how you really feel. Just know that I will be coming for my son. Now get the fuck out my place of business." She turned around and made a dramatic ass exit. I was now convinced that she was indeed crazy. I immediately picked up my phone and called Boss. He needed to get this bitch in check immediately. I couldn't afford to go back to jail for beating her motherfucking ass. It wasn't worth it. At this point, I was worried about my son and his wellbeing. I wasn't going to be okay until he was living with me and away from that crazy bitch.

*****

I sat inside White Palace Grill waiting for Boss to arrive. Ever since my verbal altercation with Meesh, my mind has been on nothing but my son. I decided not to even mention the shit to him. I just wanted to let him know that I wanted our son to move in with me.

I sat nervously waiting for him. I hadn't seen him since the night we kissed. I had talked to my son a couple of times, but we never said more than one or two words to one another. I guess he was feeling awkward as well.

"Hey, ma. I'm sorry I'm late. The traffic on Lake Shore Drive was a bitch," Boss said as he kissed me on the jaw and sat across from me. This man was fine as shit and I was mad at his momma for creating his ass. I had to pick up the menu and start fanning myself to cool down.

"It's cool. I just need to talk to you about something really important." My palms were so sweaty that I had to rub them on my pants. I hated that Boss had this type of effect on me. I feel like the father of my child is a perfect stranger. I sometimes feel like we're just getting to know each other and in a way, that's the truth.

"Is everything cool, Yonnah?" That's another thing; he made my panties wet each and every time he called me Yonnah. He had been calling me that since the moment we formally met. That shit drove me crazy.

"Everything is fine. I just wanted to know how you felt about Lil Boss coming to live with me permanently. I just moved into my new home and I want him to be there with me. I want to be more hands-on with him. It's hard with him living with you and Meesh. If you don't want that, I totally understand. After all, you're his legal guardian." I watched as Boss ran his hands over his face in deep thought.

"I'm so used to my lil nigga living with me, but I know you need to bond with him. Let's gradually do it, though. How about he comes with you every weekend and holidays until school is out. He can finish the school year out with us and then he can move in with you for good. Is that cool?"

"That's great. Thanks." I was so excited I jumped up and wrapped my arms around him. I quickly stopped once I realized what I was doing, but he quickly pulled me back into his embrace.

"Stop doing that, Yonnah. There is nothing wrong with us hugging or the kiss we shared.

However, I'm sorry that I kissed you. That wasn't cool on my part. I honestly couldn't help it. As a matter of fact, since you got out, I haven't been able to think about anything but your beautiful ass. I'm still in love with you and that's real." My breathing became labored as I struggled with his revelation. It was the moment of truth for me. I could either express my true feelings for him or cower from fear of rejection. It didn't matter that he still loved me, the fact was, he was still married, so I chose the latter.

"It's good to know that you still love me. That means everything, but the fact remains the same; you're married. I will always love you, but I'm not in love with you. I'll text you the address so that you can drop him off this weekend. Goodbye, Karion." I tried to walk away from him, but he grabbed me back and lifted my chin so that we could look into each other's eyes.

"Look at me and tell me you're not in love with me. If you can do that, I'll never bother you again. It will be strictly about Lil Boss." He licked his lips and my pussy got wet. At that moment, all I could do was think about his tatted body on top of mine and me pulling on his long ass dreads. This nigga was making it hard for me to walk away from him. Of course I was in love with him. He knew exactly what he was doing and I knew once I revealed my true feelings, there was no going back.

"I am in love with you, Boss. I'm just so scared." I didn't realize I was crying until he was wiping my tears.

"I'm the last person in the world you have to be scared of. Let's get out of here." I couldn't believe this shit. One minute we were standing in the middle of the damn restaurant, and the next on our way to the damn hotel. This is so wrong, but Boss makes it feel so right.

*****

She a winner, my favorite place is up in her

Slide in her like a splinter, might treat that pussy like dinner

Legs in the air like antennas

Then climb up on top like a wrestler, she down for the count

Hold her leg up whenever I pin her

I cut like a dealer, my baby cum, I cum with her

Take care of that box, I deliver, she wet like a river

Boss rapped the verse of "Wifin' You" by Montana of 300 in my ear as he fucked my brains out. It had been years since I had sex. I felt as though I was a virgin all over again. Before I got locked up, I was familiar with his body, but now it was so foreign to me. I was laid out on my back and he was on top of me. Boss was taking my body to heights of pleasure I never thought possible. He had my legs spread eagle and he was hitting my spot each and every time. I grabbed a hold of his butt cheeks and pulled him in closer. I wanted to feel all of him. I rested my face into the nape of his neck, inhaling the intoxicating scent of his Creed cologne.

"I missed you so much, Yonnah." Boss began to kiss me passionately.

"I miss you too. I'm about to cum," I said out of breath.

"Let that shit go, ma. Cum all over this dick right now!" On command, I came more than I realized. He pulled his dick out and all my juices began to squirt out. He put it back in, thrust inside of me with force, then pulled it out, causing me to squirt everywhere. I had never experienced anything like that before. Boss had my ass shaking like I was having a seizure. Not long after, he slipped his dick back inside of me and went in for the kill. He held onto me tight as he came inside of me. We both laid there in each other's arms, drenched in each other's sweat. I wish that I could have this moment for life, but unfortunately, it was short-lived. His phone began to ring back to back. He jumped up and rushed into the bathroom to answer it. At that moment, I regretted having sex with him. I knew that was most likely Meesh on the phone. I couldn't be mad because the fact of the matter was, she was his wife.

The sound of him arguing with her made me jump up and put my clothes on. I don't know why, but I got dressed and left the suite without telling him. There I was again, more confused than I was after our kiss. My phone began to ring over and over again. I knew that it was Boss, but I let it go straight to voicemail. I needed to get the hell away from him and quick. I needed a drink immediately. I rushed home, took a quick shower, and headed over to Shannie's house. I needed my best friend more than ever right now.

About an hour later, I pulled up to her house and I wanted to pull right back off. I watched as Boss and Meesh, along with my son, walked hand in hand up to their door. What were the odds of this shit happening? I was leaning towards pulling off, but I hadn't seen my son in about a week, so I decided to take one for the team and stay.

I took a deep breath and exited my car. I still had my set of keys, so I went inside.

"Hi, Mommy." Lil Boss ran full speed ahead towards me and wrapped his arms around my waist.

"Hey, baby. I missed you so much." I kneeled down and placed kissed all over his face. I looked up and this bitch Meesh had her face screwed up. I silently prayed that God kept her covered in the blood because she had no more chances with me. I swear I'm gone beat her ass. I'm done talking and arguing with this jealous bitch. Meesh was sitting on Boss' lap, kissing all over his lips. I wondered if she tasted my pussy. I was just riding his face like a cowgirl. Meesh was absolutely stupid. I watched this girl as she tried to bury Boss' face into her breasts so that he wouldn't be able to see me. I had so much respect for this woman while I was locked up. Now that I know the real her, that bitch gets nothing from me. I couldn't care less that she had raised my son. He had been nothing but a pawn in her quest to marry his father. I walked inside of the kitchen and Shannie was straining some pasta.

"I was just about to call you. Kartier decided to throw a BBQ all of a sudden. Did you see your little friend out front?" I rolled my eyes at Shannie while she was trying to be funny. I know she didn't know, but I was so not in the mood to be joking about this bitch Meesh.

"That bitch ain't my friend."

The sound of a car screeching and a loud crashing sound caused Shannie and me to rush out of the front door. Boss, Meesh, Kartier, and all of the rest of the kids were already out there.

"Oh my God!" My heart stopped beating when I saw Lil Boss laying in the middle of the street. Everything started to move in slow motion as I collapsed on top of his lifeless body.

Chapter 4-Boss

Seeing my lil nigga lying in the middle of the street had me fucked up. It had been about three hours since he had gone back for surgery and we hadn't heard a word since. They had us sitting in the family room of the hospital and the silence in the room was killing me. I took that time to pay attention to the interactions between Meesh and K'Yonnah. As I observed them, I knew that some things were definitely brewing between them. I knew that the shit was not going to turn out good. Meesh was being petty and territorial over both me and Lil Boss while K'Yonnah was trying her best not to show any emotions in regards to the situation. However, I knew that she was about to burst at any minute.

We were trying our best not to look at each other. I guess we were both avoiding one another due to our sexual encounter. Her ass had a nigga so gone off the pussy that I wanted more. K'Yonnah has the type of pussy that'll make a nigga go bankrupt trying to pay for the shit. My baby momma got a nigga feeling like R. Kelly, wanting to marry that pussy. I know that I probably shouldn't be thinking about that at this point in time, but anything would suffice to help the ache in my heart for my son. K'Yonnah stood up and got ready to leave out of the room, but I quickly grabbed her.

"Where are you going?"

"To the Chapel so that I can pray for our son." She wiped tears from her eyes and just seeing her crying made tears well up in mine. I had been trying to remain strong for her and everybody else, but seeing them hurt had me hurting.

"Come on, we can pray for him together." We grabbed one another's hand and headed out the door.

"I'll come too," Meesh said.

"Look, if you don't mind, we just want to pray for our son. The life that we created as one. Yes, you helped Karion raise him, but the fact remains the same that I birthed him. Please fall back, Meesh. You're doing too much for me. I allowed you to ride in the ambulance with them. I've been letting a lot of things happen out of respect that you looked out for him. At the same time, you don't like me and I don't like your ass. Karion is your husband and he's the father of my son. I know you hate it, but we share him. You can stop walking around acting like somebody wants your husband. I told your ass if I wanted him, I could have him."

"Is that true, Karion? If she wanted you, she could have you?" The room was filled with family and all eyes were on me. Right now wasn't the time or place for K'Yonnah or Meesh to be having this debate. I'm a man before I'm anything and I would never want my wife and my baby momma to be arguing and fighting with one another.

"This is not the time or place to be having this discussion. In case y'all ass forgot, my son is back there fighting for his life. I suggest both of y'all get off this bullshit with one another. Lil Boss wouldn't want his mothers acting this way."

"He only has one mother," K'Yonnah said as she walked out the door. Shannie jumped up and tried to go after her. I just shook my head and sat back down.

"Maybe I should just leave. It's obvious I'm not wanted here."

"Shut the fuck up, Meesh. Don't think I'm playing a blind eye to the shit you been on with K'Yonnah."

"I'm so sick and tired of you taking up for her ass. It seems like since she came home you've been up her ass. Maybe you two should be together. I mean, then you wouldn't have to sneak around and fuck each other. Oh, you thought I didn't know. I know you and her were at the hotel earlier today. When I called, you flat out lied to me. If you no longer want me, just be a man about it." Meesh was shedding tears and I felt bad about that. She grabbed her purse and left out of the family room. I wanted to go after her, but seconds later, the surgeon came in. I quickly stood to my feet and prepared myself to hear the news about my son's condition. As soon as he started to talk, K'Yonnah came back in. Her eyes were bloodshot red and that fucked me up. There was too much going on at the moment. I just needed the doctor to tell me my son was going to be okay so that I could sit down and have a talk with the two most important women in my life.

"Mr. and Mrs. Miller, I just want you to know that the surgery was a success. Karion did great. We were able to repair his broken collarbone and his leg. We had to remove his spleen because it was so badly damaged. He will be able to live a good life without it. With physical therapy, he will be back up and walking in no time. We'll keep him for a couple of days and then he can go home. He will need around the clock care due to the upper body cast. I can't begin to tell you how lucky he is. He is a trooper. You guys can come back and see him shortly."

"Thank you so much," K'Yonnah said as she wiped the tears from her eyes. He simply smiled and nodded before walking off.

"We're going to go ahead and get up out of here, bro. I'll call you in a little while," Kartier said as we dapped it up. Shannie and K'Yonnah hugged one another.

"Thanks, bro, for coming. You too, sis," I said and they left. I quickly turned around and focused on K'Yonnah, who rolled her eyes and swiftly walked away. She was gone have to do something about that attitude because Lil Boss did not need to be around all of that negative ass energy.

"Before we head back, let me holla at you for a minute." I grabbed K'Yonnah by her arm and walked her over to the chairs so that we could sit and talk.

"I'm really not in the mood, Karion. I just want to go back here and check on my baby." She tried to pull away, but I had to grab her ass back forcibly. I had never been this way with her, but I had to be at this moment. I'm not about to play with her ass either.

"I really don't give a fuck what you in the mood for. Now let's get some shit straight. I know you in your feelings about what happened between us, but I don't regret the shit. Stop walking around with an attitude like I did something to you. All I did was put this dick in your life and it fucked you up in the head. I understand all of that. Now it's obvious some shit has happened between you and Meesh and I wasn't informed, so enlighten me. I simply cannot deal with the bullshit y'all on right now. The only thing that matters is Lil Boss. Talk to me, Yonnie. What's on your mind?" She was sitting, looking through her phone, acting uninterested, so I snatched it out of her hand.

"I don't have an attitude with you. I'm just sick of your wife walking around here like her role in my son's life is more important than mine. At the same time, I don't want to be beefing with this bitch over her husband. I heard what she said before I walked back in here. That shit was embarrassing hearing her say that shit out in the open like that. It makes me look like a fucking home wrecker, even though she has been accusing me of wanting you since the moment I came home. I don't want any parts in fucking up your marriage. I regret that we had sex; it has me feelings things I shouldn't. Let's just act like it never happened. Can I go back here and see my son now?"

"I'm not going to act like it never happened because it did. It fucks me up to know that you regret it. Out of everything I've regretted in my life, you've never been one of them. I'm glad I know how you really feel. From this moment forward, I promise I won't come at you on anything else besides being Lil Boss' pops. If you need me, you know that I'm here without a doubt. I've even decided to let Lil Boss come live with you permanently. No matter what, you're his mother and I don't like you feeling like this. I'll handle Meesh. Let's go back here and see our son." I hated it, but I had to fall back from K'Yonnah on a personal level. Having sex only further complicated things. I truly didn't regret what had transpired between us. That shit had a nigga sprung, but the fact remained the same; I'm married. I should never have taken it there out of respect for my wife. Meesh has been a good wife to me and she doesn't deserve the shit I've done. However, I won't deny that there is something in my heart and soul for K'Yonnah.

I feel shit for K'Yonnah that I shouldn't feel. It's better if I just steer clear and be a father to my son. She has regrets and I'm bitter about that, almost to the point where I want to snap the fuck out, but I can't. As a man, I have to respect K'Yonnah's wishes. Our friendship means more to me than anything in this world and I don't want to lose that with her. I don't know who has me fucked up in the head more—her or Meesh. Now that I've handled this shit with K'Yonnah, I need to head home and talk with Meesh. I already know it won't be pretty.

Chapter 5- Meesh

Tears blinded my vision as I drove home to the house that I shared with Karion. My feelings were beyond hurt. All day I had been trying my best to hold all of my feelings inside, especially after Lil Boss was hit by a car. I know that I'm frowned upon due to my behavior with K'Yonnah. I didn't mean to be so mean and hateful towards her, but I know that she still loves my husband. I also know that he loves her. At first, I thought that I was indeed over exaggerating, but then I started to notice a change in him when we were in her presence. Boss and I have been together for almost five years and married for three. During this time, I know that he has cheated with other women, but it never came to our doorstep. I've never had to deal with another woman. I've always been comfortable in my position as his wife.

He's never given me a reason to feel threatened by another woman, but things have changed in such a short period of time. The moment K'Yonnah was released from prison, things changed. No, let me rephrase that; Boss changed. I can feel it in the way he looks at me and the way he touches me. Boss loved K'Yonnah and the way he catered to her fucked me up in the head.

The only reason I went and said that shit to K'Yonnah was because Boss came home with lipstick all over him. I knew it was her lipstick. I guess in a way I was wrong because I should have addressed him. That made me less of a woman. Then today I actually followed him and her to the hotel. When he told me she called so that they could meet up and discuss something, I had a funny ass feeling about it all. So, I came to the restaurant and stayed outside in an Uber so that he wouldn't notice my car.

When they both came out of the restaurant and got inside of the car, I decided to follow them further. My heart dropped when I saw them holding hands and walking into the hotel. Instead of following him inside, I went home. I called him and asked him where he was and he lied. I knew then we would never be the same. I couldn't bring myself to say anything when he came home and said that we were going over to his brother's house. I just agreed to go. Lil Boss getting hitting by that car happened so fast. He's my son and I don't care what anyone says. I might not be his biological mother, but I've been here when he needed me most. It was me who sat up with him all night when he had the colic. I was the one who took him for shots and nursed his achy legs and fevers. Boss was out in the streets hanging out and coming in at all times of night. Say what the fuck you want to say about me, but I deserve some type of respect from both Boss and K'Yonnah.

I felt myself sinking back into depression and I was trying my best not to take the Zoloft my doctor had prescribed. I disliked the way it made me feel. Plus, I was pregnant again and too afraid to tell Boss. Mainly because I knew that he was dead set against it. I had already had two miscarriages in one year. Both times I miscarried at four months. I always carry small so one could never tell that I was actually pregnant. I'm at the twelve-week mark and I've been doing good so far. I plan on telling Boss after and if I pass the sixteen-week mark. I know that I will have to deal with the repercussions and consequences of lying about taking my birth control. I had long ago thrown that shit in the garbage. Call me crazy, but I had every intention of having a baby with my husband. This has nothing to do with K'Yonnah or Lil Boss. Every wife wants to give her husband a child and I'll die trying to do it. Boss is everything to me and that's why I'm so hurt. He's all that I have and I know he's going to leave me for her. I might as well do whatever I need to do to hold on to him.

A part of me wanted to wild out, but I decided to take the high road and behave like a woman about this. I needed Boss to tell me the truth and hoped that we could move on from this. I know I sound crazy, but I just don't want to lose him to her. I absolutely meant my vows when I said them before God and our families. I'm not giving up on my marriage that easy. So, it's till death do us part and trust me when I say, I'll kill him and die in the process to keep him from being with her.

Chapter 6- K'Yonnah

If you look in my life you'll see what I see

Oh you'll see that I'm so blue!!

The soulful sounds of Mary J. Blige's "My Life" had me all in my feelings. I swear Mary had a song for every damn situation a woman could go through. The Chardonnay mixed with her lyrics had me yearning for Boss, but I hadn't seen him since Meesh revealed to the whole damn emergency room that he and I had fucked. That shit was so embarrassing. The last thing I wanted to do was come off as a home wrecker, but his dick was so good. It was even better than what I remembered before I got locked up. The fact remained the same he was married to her and I wanted no parts of that situation. I refused to play the mistress to any nigga. I keep hearing him professing his love for me while we fucked, but as soon as she called, he jumped out of bed and rushed into the bathroom, explaining himself. I wasn't beat for having to be quiet while a man talked to his wife on the phone; as a woman, that shit is so beneath you. I love Boss, but the best decision I ever made was telling him to stay away from me. Even if it does hurt like hell. Being intimate with him after all these years brought back so many feelings that I thought were gone. Actually, they were never gone, I just placed them deep inside of me. I had no other choice with him getting married and all. The shit is actually hard to suppress looking at our son every day. No matter what, I had to stand firm in my decision to cut off personal ties with Boss. My heart has been through enough and I can't take any more heartbreak. We both needed to focus on just being parents to our son.

It had been a month since Lil Boss was hit by the car and I hadn't had a moment's rest. Doctor appointments and physical therapy had been taking up all my time. I was so grateful that I had Shannie; she had been running my center in my absence. I now had three women and their children staying there and I was so excited about it. Not excited that they were being abused, but the fact that I could help someone get out of an abusive relationship.

I never thought I would ever get out of Stone's stronghold. I also never thought I would do time for killing his ass. It's imperative that I help women who are in domestic violence situations. I never want anyone to go through what I did. I'm out of prison, but I suffer daily. My life is still not normal. Jail can be a very traumatic experience. I had my good days and my bad days. I'm just glad I was able to do my time and get home to my baby. I just hate that I feel so institutionalized. There are days I have to remind myself that I'm no longer in prison. It's like my body is programmed to get up at the crack of dawn and I'm so obsessive compulsive these days. Shit has to be clean and organized or I can't function. The shit drives Shannie crazy when we're at work. I think I'll need to see some type of psychologist because it's starting to drive me crazy.

I was sitting in my office reading over proposals and grants from the State. I was trying to get all of the government funding I could for my center. All my savings had been damn near depleted building my center and buying my house. I was low on cash, but I wasn't broke.

"Girl, let's go to happy hour and have some drinks," Shannie said as she walked into my office and sat down.

"I'm swamped, girl. After I finish sending off all of these forms, I'm going home and get in bed. Plus, Boss is bringing my baby home today. I've missed him so much."

"I called Boss and told him to drop my god baby over to my house because I've missed him. Give that boy some air. He's recovering just fine. It's Friday, K'Yonnah. You need to get out and have a drink and possibly get you some dick. I know your ass got cobwebs on that pussy." Before I could respond, Boss appeared in the doorway of my office. The look on his face showed me that he had heard what Shannie said.

"H-heyy!" I stammered.

"Can I have a minute with my baby momma, sis?" He was biting the inside of his jaw and I knew that meant he was mad. I hoped it wasn't because of what Shannie said. He had a whole wife at home. He needed to channel his anger over to her ass. Shannie looked at me and made a funny face before walking out.

"Of course, bro. We're going out, Yonnah, and I'm not taking no for an answer." I shook my head at her and gestured for Karion to come inside.

"Is everything okay with Lil Boss?"

"He's fine, Yonnah. I just needed to see you. I got some shit going on and I need a woman's point of view." I looked at him strangely because if needs a woman's perspective, he should be talking to his wife.

"What's on your mind, Karion?"

"Karion, huh?"

"That's your name, ain't it?"

"Whatever, K'Yonnah." He shook his head like he was so upset that I called him by his government name. This nigga needs to hurry up and get out of my office. He was sitting across from me looking good as fuck all stressed out and shit. My pussy was doing jumps, flips and all types of other shit. I squeezed my legs together trying to keep my juices from leaking out. I hated how much power Boss had over my kitty kat. You know a nigga the shit if he can make you cum from his presence alone.

"So what brings you over here, Baby Daddy."

"Don't call me that shit. I'm the father of your son."

"Well, excuse me then. I was just joking." He was being all serious and shit.

"My bad, but I don't like to be called that shit. Only whack ass niggas don't mind being called baby daddy. I'm a Boss, and more importantly, a father."

"Yes, you are a wonderful father and I'm so grateful for you. Now, why the hell are you here acting like someone pissed in your cereal?"

"Shit so crazy, Yonnah. This morning I found some paperwork from Meesh's doctor. It said that she was pregnant." He rubbed his hand over his face in frustration and I really didn't understand why he looked like it was the end of the world. I was taken aback as to why he was telling me this because I was low-key jealous.

"That's great. You should be happy. You guys have been trying for some time now."

"That's the thing. Meesh knows that it's too risky for her to be trying to have a baby so soon. Not only that, she's hiding the shit from me. I read the paperwork and it said she was in her second trimester. Meesh's ass knows I didn't want her to get pregnant because I feared her losing it. That's why she's hiding it from me. I want to be happy, but I'm too fucking pissed at the fact that she's being sneaky and underhanded about the shit. I hate people who lie to me; that shit rubs me the wrong way." Boss was all in his feelings and I was looking at him like he was crazy, but I needed to get him out of my office because I wanted to fuck him right there in my office.

"I think that you should go home and talk to your wife about this. I'm sure there's a logical explanation. You have to give her a chance to explain herself." I raised up from my chair and got ready to walk over to the file cabinet to put away the work that I was working on. When I turned around, Boss was blocking me from walking past. I slowly backed up into the wall. He wasn't saying a word, he was just staring at me intensely and lustfully. He leaned in and kissed me on the lips. I hated that I moaned out in pleasure from his kiss alone. As we engaged in a passionate kiss, his hands roamed down my body, lifting my skirt up. I could have stopped him, but I didn't. He roughly snatched my panties off and lifted me on top of the short file cabinet. He gently pushed me back and buried his face in my pussy. As soon as his tongue flicked across my clit, I moaned out in pleasure as he sucked and licked on me.

"Fuckkkkk!" I yelled out as I gripped the sides of the file cabinet, trying to get some balance. My pussy was dripping like a faucet and I was sliding from my juices.

"You taste so fucking good, Yonnah." He stood up and wiped my juices from his mouth. He pulled down his black joggers and his Polo boxers. His dick was standing at attention and I just started shaking my head no.

"Boss, we can't keep doing this." He grabbed me by my hand and led me over to the loveseat I had in the room.

"I need you right now, Yonnah. I'm gone go crazy if I can't feel the inside. Please, ma, just make love to a nigga for old time's sake." He looked so damn pitiful and sexy at the same time. Not to mention his dick had me in a trance just staring at it. He had these veins protruding from the shaft that made my mouth water. I threw caution to the wind and decided to take control of the situation. I pushed him down on the seat and straddled him.

"Mmmmmmmm!" I moaned out in pleasure as I slid down on his dick with ease. He gripped my waist and began to slam me down viciously on his dick. I wrapped my arms around him and held onto him for dear life. There I was thinking I was about to take over, but this nigga bossed up on my pussy quick.

"Would you bring ya– Ooops, I'm sorry!" Shannie had burst in my office and caught our asses. One would think we would have stopped, but we didn't. Shannie quickly walked back out.

"Cum on this dick, Yonnah!"

"Oh shittttt! I'm cumming!"

"Ahhhhhhhh!" he hollered and shook as he came as well. That shit was so powerful and orgasmic. I tried to raise up, but he quickly pulled me back down.

"I have to go, Boss. This shit is crazy. I'm fucking you in my office and this shit is wrong." I don't know why, but I couldn't look in his face at the moment. A part of me was so ashamed of my actions. Boss made this shit feel so good, but as a woman, it was very wrong.

"Why the fuck do you keep saying this shit is wrong?"

"It's wrong because your ass is married, nigga, or did you forget!" I pulled away from him and started fixing my clothes. He stood to his feet and pulled his clothes up as well.

"First of all, watch the tone of your voice, K'Yonnah. Second, stop reminding me that I'm married because I'm very well aware of it."

"Act like it then." I rushed into my personal washroom that was inside my office and slammed the door behind me. I placed my back up against the door and closed my eyes tight. Having sex with Boss was becoming too much for me. Yes, the shit felt good as fuck, but once we were finished, I felt like shit. Mainly because I knew that he was going back home to his wife. As a woman, that shit makes me feel so low. It doesn't matter that we have a bond and a child together. I still feel like a bitch on the street who just got used. I know it sounds crazy, but that's how I feel. I shook my head hearing my office door slam. I was happy as hell Boss had left. I simply couldn't walk out and look him in the face. I feel like a little ass girl around this nigga. What the fuck is wrong with me?

Chapter 7- Shannie

I was completely confused as I sat across from K'Yonnah at Margaritaville. She had been quiet as a church mouse since we had been inside of the restaurant. I know that she might be a little embarrassed about me walking in on her riding the shit out of Boss, but she has no reason to be. I'm rooting for those two to get back together so I have no idea why she's acting like this. I don't want to be a bad friend, but right now, I need K'Yonnah to get the fuck out of her feelings because this Debbie Downer ass shit is starting to get on my nerves.

"Are you just going to sit there and sulk over this shit?"

"I'm not sulking, Shannie. I just have a lot of shit on my plate right now. I'm worried like crazy thinking about my son and his recovery. Not to mention this shit going on with Boss. My head is literally all over the place. Did you forget you just caught us having sex? That shit was so embarrassing." K'Yonnah shook her head and placed her face in the palm of her hands.

"How could I forget? Your ass was riding the shit out that nigga." We both laughed and I was happy to at least see her smile.

"Girl, I keep telling myself I'm not gone fuck him anymore, but every time he comes around me, I'm dropping my damn panties. That shit is not a good look on my part." K'Yonnah grabbed her peach margarita and sipped it.

"Please enlighten me. Why isn't it a good look on your part? You love him and I know for a fact he loves you."

"That's true, but the fact remains the same that nigga is married. As much as I love him, I can't keep letting him play mind games with me. One minute he wants to be laid up fucking me, then the next he's jumping up to go home to his wife. Today he comes in my office talking about how she's pregnant and all that shit. I don't give a fuck about her being pregnant. Apparently, she's hiding the shit from him. I'm lost as to why he thought I would want to hear the shit. I'm not his fucking go-to girl when shit ain't going good on the home front. That nigga's dick game is the truth, but it ain't good enough to make me comfortable with playing the side bitch to a nigga I was with before he got married. I'm good on that nigga. Meesh needs to tend to her fucking husband so he can leave me alone."

"I totally understand. If this shit got you all in your feelings like this, then bitch your ass is going to have to have more willpower than you have. I'm married to his brother, so trust and believe me I know that the struggle is real. You've been out of jail some time now, so it's time we get you back on the dating scene. I know that you've only been with Stone and Boss, but it's time you get you a boo thang."

"I don't have time for a man in my life. I just want to focus on building a relationship with my son and my organization." With that being said, I left it at that. K'Yonnah was headstrong, so I knew she meant everything she said about not wanting to deal with a man right now. I hated that Stone hurt her and I felt so sad that Boss got married while she was away. K'Yonnah had been trying her best to be strong but it's wearing her down tremendously, but I have faith that she will be okay. She and Boss were meant to be. In my heart, I know that they will be together. I knew it from the moment I first saw how they looked at each other years back when she was staying with me. I don't know what it is. I just know that they will get their happily ever after.

After sipping a couple more margaritas, I was nice and tipsy. All I wanted to do was go home and lay up under Kartier. We barely get any quality time together. With me working at the center full-time, and him running his businesses, we never really have time for one another. Not to mention being full-time parents. We absolutely had to start making time for us.

*****

When I pulled into my driveway, I was surprised to see that Kartier wasn't home, especially since he had our kids and Lil Boss. He had most likely taken them out for ice cream or something. I decided to take that time to soak in a hot bath and relax. As soon as I got undressed, my doorbell rang. I quickly threw on something and rushed down the stairs to answer the door. I looked through the peephole and saw that it was Nikkita. She was a good friend of his. I had met her a couple of times when we first got together, but soon after, she moved away.

"Hi, Nikki. Kartier is not home now. Can I help you with anything?"

"I'm actually here to see you, Shannie."

"Come inside. I'm sorry, I was just about to take a bath. What's going on?" I gestured for her to sit on the sofa and I sat across from her on the loveseat.

"I don't know how to tell you this, so I'm just going to come out and tell you. Kartier and I have a six-year-old daughter named Paris. Before you and him met, we were messing around. When you first got with him, we continued to have a sexual relationship, which produced my daughter... our daughter. He was furious when he found out that I was pregnant because at that point, he was in love with you and wanted no parts of me or her. It hurt me to the core and I couldn't bear to see you guys together, so I picked up and moved away to Texas. I'm sorry about all of this, Shannie. It has never been my intention to hurt you or Kartier. The only reason I'm here is because I fear for the safety of my daughter and mine as well. I need you and Kartier to get her for me just until I can get out of this dangerous situation I'm in. I can't let him hurt her anymore." I was stunned in silence and shocked hearing this woman tell me that she had a daughter with my husband. I had never been speechless in my life, but this shit had me mute.

"Bae! Whose car is that outside? There's a little girl in there sleep." Kartier walked in but quickly stopped in his tracks when he saw the answer to his question sitting in our living room. The look in his eyes let me know that Nikkita was telling the truth about them sharing a child. I was hurt because he knew, but never told me. I was disappointed because he said fuck his daughter for me. I would never be the type of woman who kept a man from his child. I love Kartier with my heart and soul, but right now, I feel so betrayed. There's nothing like being kept in the dark about shit like this. I feel like I've been made a fool out of. I lie next to my husband every night and think that I know him. Right now, I feel like I've been sleeping next to a fucking stranger for six years.

"I'm sorry, Kartier. I'm not trying to ruin your life, but I need you to get our daughter. I'm in a fucked up place right now and I need you. I've never asked for anything, nor have I insisted you be in her life, even though the DNA test proved that you are her father. I've never come at you crazy. If my back wasn't up against the wall, I swear I wouldn't be here. Please, Kartier, I need your help!" I was so disgusted hearing the detail about the DNA test, I was officially done. I took my sleeping daughter from his arms and ushered Lil Boss and Baby K up the stairs and away from all of this confusion. I heard the doorbell chime and I rushed over to my bedroom window. My heart sank as I observed Nikkita and Kartier outside in a heated argument. A part of me wanted to rush out there and hear what was being said, but I was too afraid to hear more shit about their secret affair and the child they had together. I had heard enough revelations for the day. My heart couldn't take anymore. I laid across my bed and stared at the ceiling. Never in a million years did I ever think a woman would come to my home and reveal the fact that she and my husband shared a child. This shit was too much for me at the moment.

It's like I should be tearing shit up and acting a fool, but after all of that, he will still have a baby with this woman, so it would be a waste of energy.

Chapter 8- Kartier

The moment I walked inside the crib, I wanted to run my ass out of the house. Seeing Nikkita talking to Shannie had a nigga shook and I don't scare easily. The disgusted look on Shannie's face let me know that she knew about my daughter Paris. I know shit is looking real fucked up on my end. It wasn't that I didn't want to take care of my responsibility, I just didn't want it to change Shannie's mind about being with a nigga. I had been with plenty of women in my lifetime, but none of them compared to her. From the first time I laid eyes on her I knew that I wanted her to be my wife and bear my children. Just when shit was going right for me, Nikkita dropped a bomb on me about being pregnant. From the jump, I questioned her because we were just fuck buddies, nothing major. Nikkita up and moved out of town on a nigga right after the DNA test proved she was my daughter. She was also in her feelings about me not wanting Shannie to know. I was dead set against Shannie knowing about Paris. Nikkita was in her feelings about that and me getting married to Shannie, so she wanted her daughter to have no parts of us. I respected her wishes but took care of my responsibilities. I've been sending checks to Nikkita's mother for Paris because I had no clue where Nikkita was. The only thing that's wrong with all of this is the fact that I kept this shit from my wife. Not to mention the fact that I've denied my daughter the chance to know her father.

******

"Why the fuck would you show up at my crib, Nikkita?"

"Listen to me, Kartier. I swear I wouldn't be here if I didn't have to. Please just hear me out. I'm not here to cause any problems with you and Shannie. I just don't know where else to go." Nikkita was trembling and crying. I could tell that something was really wrong.

"Step outside and let's talk." She wiped the tears from her face and followed me outside.

"Momma, I woke up and you were gone. I was scared." I looked into the face of the little girl and I felt like shit. It was as if I was staring at my twin. She looked more like me than my kids with Shannie. Shit was creepy as fuck. Not to mention, awkward as hell. She was staring at me with narrow eyes; it was as if she was reading my soul or something.

"I'm sorry. I just needed to come and see a friend. Roll up the window. We can leave in a minute."

"Hurry up. I'm hungry and sleepy."

"What's going on, Nikkita? Why you got her out here sleep in a car? No, let me rephrase that.

What the hell is going on in your life that you showed up on my doorstep unannounced?"

"I had to leave Texas because I was being abused by my husband, Cord. I could take him hitting me, but not her. I think he broke her arm. She keeps saying that she fell off her bike, but I just feel like there's something more to it. When he went to sleep yesterday morning, I hopped on the road and drove here. My mother doesn't even know that I'm here. I don't want her around him. I swear, Kartier, that nigga is ruthless and he's one of the biggest kingpins in Dallas. He's going to come after me or send his goonies. He's going to kill me for leaving him."

"Stop crying, Nikkita. Let me figure all of this out. Here is two thousand dollars. Go downtown to the Hilton and book a room for you guys for the week; charge whatever you want to the room. Here's my phone number. Call me as soon as you guys get settled. I need to sit down and talk this over with Shannie. I'll come by the hotel and we can work some things out, but you have to know this is going to be so hard on my wife."

"Thanks, Kartier. I swear I'm not here to hurt her or you. After all of this is over, we'll be out of yall's hair and you never have to worry about us again. But right now, I need you and Shannie to look out for my baby until I can get all of this handled."

"We'll talk about it later." I pulled her in for a hug because I could tell that she needed it. She was genuine with her words. However, if I think she's on some bullshit, I'm going to kill her ass and that's on my life. I stood in the driveway and watched as she pulled off. I took a deep breath and headed back into the house. I slowly made my way up the stairs and to our bedroom. The door was closed, but I could hear Shannie sniffling. That shit hurt me to the core because all of this shit could have been prevented. At the time, I was being selfish and not thinking of how this could affect us in the long run.

I walked inside and Shannie quickly wiped her the tears from her face.

"Look, bae, I'm—"

"Let me stop your ass right there. I don't need you coming in here saying that you're sorry because no apology will suffice for this shit. I'm hurt, I'm mad, I'm embarrassed, and most importantly, I feel betrayed. Do you have any idea how I just felt opening the door for the mother of your child that I didn't know existed? Here I am walking around with the firm belief that I was the only woman who had given you children. We've been together for six years and you've been keeping this secret from me all along. Here I was thinking that I know you, but I don't, Kartier. You're a stranger. We vowed to spend the rest of our lives together. For better or for worse and I take my vows serious. As bad as I want to fuck you up and put you the fuck out of my house, I won't. After I'm done doing all of that, the fact will still remain that you have a daughter with Nikkita. I love you and I have to accept her because she is a part of you, but I'm telling you right now if I find out that there is some fishy shit going on with you and that bitch, I'm going to kill your black ass and hers too. Don't fuck with me, Kartier. I'm giving you the green light to help Nikkita with Paris because just looking at Nikkita, I can tell there is something bigger than what she's letting on. Step the fuck up and see what the hell is going on with your daughter."

"I don't even know what to say or do, Shannie."

"Don't say shit. There's nothing to say. Just do what you need to do for your daughter. If Nikkita feels like she needs to leave her here with us, then so be it, but you will explain to our kids about this long lost sister. Oh yeah, take your shit into the guest room. I refuse to sleep next to a liar and a fucking stranger." Shannie had surprised the shit out of me with the damn tongue action she had just given me. She had always been so mild mannered with me and never quick with her temper. I guess this is cause for her to snap out. I'm not even mad that she ain't fucking with me right now. I can breathe a breath of fresh air because I just knew Shannie was going to be talking divorce behind this shit. I grabbed me some items and headed towards the guest bedroom. When I laid down, I couldn't help but think about what the hell my next move was going to be in regards to Paris and Nikkita. I needed to do what the fuck was right in regards to my daughter. Her fucking arm is broken and shit behind some nigga who's beating Nikkita's ass. Lord knows I'm not trying to do any prison time, but I will kill this motherfucker if he hurt her in any way. Besides that, I don't know shit about baby mama drama. That's Boss' damn department. I don't want my damn wife and baby momma at each other's throats, so we without a doubt have to come to a compromise. Shannie is not playing about killing Nikkita and me, so her ass better be keeping this shit one hundred. She won't have to worry about Shannie; she's going to have to worry about me choking the life out of her ass like Tommy did Holly's ass on that TV show *Power*.

My head was all over the place and I definitely needed some advice and Boss was just the person I needed to talk to. It's funny how I'm the older brother and need to go to him for some damn guidance. It's funny how things change.

*****

"Nigga, I told you to tell Shannie about this shit a long time ago," Boss said as we sat knocking back shots of Remy at our headquarters.

"Man, bro. I know. I swear I should've listened to you. I just didn't want to lose Shannie before we walked down the fucking aisle. You know that's my baby and the last thing I ever wanted to do was hurt her. I swear, bro, I damn near shitted on the floor seeing Nikkita sitting on the couch across from Shannie.

"I'm surprised Sis didn't shoot your ass."

"Me too. I'm just glad she's allowing me to do the right thing by my daughter. It's been a long time coming and I really need to make up for lost time with my daughter. Enough about my shit. Have you told Meesh you know about her being pregnant?" I watched as my brother ran his hand over his face in frustration. This shit with Meesh was really taking a toll on him. The shit was understandable. Her ass knows she can't handle carrying a baby. Right now she's just being spiteful so that she can have one up on K'Yonnah.

"I can't even bring myself to talk to her or look at her for that matter. I love my wife, but her keeping this shit from me has me looking at her different. We're supposed to be a team and she's making decisions for both of us. Meesh knows this shit is a bad idea. As much as I'm against it, I have to support my wife. Even though I don't agree with it, I know that this is something she longs for. I just hope and pray everything works out because I can't take another loss, bro."

"Everything is going to be just fine, bro." I reached over and patted him on the shoulder. At the same time, my phone began to chime and it was an incoming call from what I knew to be Nikkita's number.

"Yooooo!"

"Pleaseee hurry up and come to the hotel. He knows that I'm here. Oh my God! He's going to kill me!"

"Calm down, I'm on my way. Call down to the front desk and tell them not to allow anyone up but me. I'm on my way. Come roll with me, bro." I raised up and grabbed my Glock off the table.

"What's good, bro?"

"You strapped?"

"Always," he said, tapping his waist.

"I need to head over to the hotel where Nikkita and Paris are. Apparently, the nigga that's been whooping her found out where she was and threatened her."

"Say no more my nigga."

With that being said, we headed over to the hotel to see what the fuck was good with Nikkita. For the sake of this nigga, he better hope I don't catch his ass.

About twenty minutes later, we made it to the hotel and I observed Nikkita with some tall ass nigga, ushering her and Paris towards a white Benz.

"Hold up my nigga! Where the fuck you going with them?" I quickly grabbed Paris by her good arm and pushed her behind me.

"Back up. This shit ain't got nothing to do with you." He tried to reach around and grab Paris. Before I could react, Boss upped his gun and pressed it to his head.

"As a matter of fact, it has everything to do with him fuck nigga!"

"No, Boss. Please, it's cool. Just take Paris with you, Kartier! I'm going to be okay."

"Hell no! Bring your ass on too." I went to grab her ass, but she pushed me away and moved closer to him.

"Go, Kartier!" I just shook my head at this bitch.

"No, Momma. Come on. I don't want you to go with him."

"It's okay, Paris baby. Go with your daddy and your uncle Boss."

"Fuck this shit, bro. If she wants to go with this nigga, let her go, but she won't be taking Paris with her." I picked my daughter up and got ready to walk the fuck away.

"This ain't over my nigga!" he yelled.

"You don't want no smoke, my nigga, but I'll be waiting whenever ya bitch ass ready!" Boss said as we walked away with Paris in tow. Nikkita had to be willing to get away from that bitch ass nigga on her own. In the meantime, Paris was coming home with me and Shannie. It would take some adjusting, but we had to do it. I just hoped shit wasn't really hard on Shannie. Saying shit was cool was different than actually dealing with it.

Chapter 9- Boss

It had been well over a month since I found out that Meesh was indeed pregnant. She was starting to show, but was still trying to hide the shit from me. I had sat on the shit for so long and was indeed ready to call her ass out on her bullshit. Before I did that, I decided to go and talk to my OG. She has always been that voice of reason when I didn't know what to do. She had been here for us during the other miscarriages. I don't know if I would be able to make it without her love and support.

"You got it smelling good up in here, Ma," I said as I walked into the kitchen and kissed her on the cheek.

"I knew you were coming over so I decided to make some of your favorite foods: meatloaf, collard greens, baked macaroni, and corn bread."

"Is it Jiffy Mix? You know I hate hot water cornbread."

"Of course it's Jiffy. How come you didn't bring Meesh and my grandson over? She loves my meatloaf."

"Lil Boss is with K'Yonnah this weekend. Meesh is at home figuring out new ways to hide her pregnancy from me." I didn't mean to say it all sarcastic like that, but I couldn't help it. The look on my mom's face was one of worry because she knew Meesh wasn't ready for this. After all, she was in the room when the doctor told her she should wait at least a full year before trying for another baby.

"Now Meesha knows it's too soon, Son. How come you guys weren't on any birth control?"

"That's the thing, Ma. She had to stop taking her pills on purpose. I have been adamant about her not getting pregnant right now. We had a conversation about this and she promised that she would wait. It's like ever since K'Yonnah came home, Meesh has been acting out and doing all type of shit for attention."

"First of all, watch your damn mouth. Second of all, Meesh ain't no fool; she knows that you're still in love with K'Yonnah. Not to mention, still having sex with her. That shit is wrong on so many levels. Now don't get me wrong, you know that I love K'Yonnah as if she were my own, but I'm a woman before I'm anything and I have to call it like I see it. She is wrong for having sex with you while you're married to Meesh. I know that you love Meesh, but I also know that you're in love with K'Yonnah. Son, listen to me and listen to me good. Stop this thing you have going on with K'Yonnah. You're a married man so you're just as much at fault as she is. Not to mention it isn't fair to her either. I know that girl is still in love with you. All of this bed hopping will lead to nothing but heartache and pain. Go home to your wife and get ready for the baby to come. I have a good feeling about this, son." I sat at my mother's table in deep thought, taking in everything that she had said and I knew it was the truth. K'Yonnah always went crazy on me after we would have sex and I knew it was because she loved me, she just didn't want to admit it to herself. The best thing would be for me to focus on Meesh and her health. I know my wife wants nothing more but to give me a baby. I just have to keep the faith that God will see us through and bless us with a healthy baby.

******

"I'm sorry I hid it from you. I knew that you would make me get an abortion." Meesh was sitting in the middle of the bed Indian-style crying.

"I would have never made you get a fucking abortion. My issue is that you went behind my back and stopped taking your birth control. You basically trapped me, Meesh."

"You're my husband. What the fuck you mean trapped you?"

"Lower your voice. I didn't mean it the way it sounded. However, you lied about some shit that was serious and detrimental to our relationship. We discussed this and we both agreed that now was not the time to have a baby. You're putting your life and the baby's life at risk. We have Lil Boss. Isn't he enough?"

"No! He's not enough. Lil Boss belongs to you and K'Yonnah. Not me. I want to give birth to my own child. I'm so sorry I kept this from you, but I had to. I'm six months, Karion. Everything is going to be okay. We've never made it past the four-month mark. I have a feeling that our daughter is going to make it and be just fine." Meesh raised up from the bed and placed my hand on her stomach.

"A girl, huh?"

"Yes. I found out last month. I'm sorry you weren't there with me. Karion, I just want to give you a baby. That would make me so happy. All I want to do is make our marriage complete. I just want you to love me like you love K'Yonnah."

"Look at me, Meesh. I do love you. Stop comparing yourself to K'Yonnah. You guys are totally different women, so I love you both in different ways. I love you because you are my wife and I love K'Yonnah because we have history and she is the mother of my son." I had to grab Meesh and look at her square in the eye to let her know I was being truthful. I love my wife and I know it might seem like I don't, but I do. However, I love K'Yonnah too. Being married to Meesh or any other woman won't change that. At the same time, I know that I have to love K'Yonnah from a distance because it's hurting my wife. The last thing I want is for her to be stressed out over feeling inadequate in regards to K'Yonnah. Plus, I don't need the added stress. I have a lot of shit going on in these streets and I need a clear and level head.

"Are you a little happy about the baby?" Meesh wrapped her arms around my neck and placed a soft kiss on my lips.

"Of course I'm happy. I'm just worried as hell."

"God got us, bae. Everything is going to be okay." Meesh's eyes were lighting up and I couldn't help but smile. I needed to let my worry subside because God had given us another chance. Instead of thinking bad shit, I decided to switch gears and focus on making this pregnancy the easiest ever for her. I couldn't wait to meet my daughter. I wanted to spoil her and treat her like the princess that she will be.

"We need to get a bigger house. This house isn't big enough for us and the kids. Princess is going to need a whole wing to her damn self."

"I love this house, Boss. You built it from the ground up for me. I don't want to leave it."

"We can keep it, Meesh, but we will be moving. End of discussion." I kissed her on the forehead and headed out of the room. I needed to get in touch with the realtor. It was a must we be moved into a new and bigger house. I still had my reservations about this, but I was also elated to be having a daughter.

Chapter 10- K'Yonnah

I couldn't believe I was visiting my daughter's grave. It was the very first time I had been there. As I looked back, I wish I had been stronger and stayed the duration of her services. As her mother, I should have stayed to see her being lowered into the Earth. Every day I beat myself up for not being stronger for her. Maybe had I been stronger and called the police when Stone took her, then she would still be here. It's like her life was snatched before she was ever able to live. I blame myself every day for being so weak.

Her grave was so neat and pretty. There were even fresh flowers. That was odd. Who would come and keep her grave so neat? I know damn well Stone's mother or sister didn't. They made it perfectly clear that they hated me for killing Stone. I didn't care about his mother hating me because I hated her ass. On the other hand, I hated that I hurt his sister. She was the only one who spoke up for me when he would beat my ass.

"Hi, Sister," Lil Boss said and kissed her grave.

"How do you know that this is your sister?" I had never even brought up the subject of him having a sister prior to bringing him to the cemetery to visit.

"Daddy and me come all the time and put flowers on her grave. Daddy says it's our job to keep it looking pretty because you couldn't." I had to hold back the tears hearing my son say that. Boss is just full of surprises and he has always been that way. I think that's what made me love him back then. He took care of me when I was someone else's woman. I loved Boss from the moment he picked me up after Stone knocked me on my ass in the middle of the street. I knew I was in love with him when he whisked me away from my daughter's funeral service and flew me to New York just to make me feel better. He's always been that nigga. Realest nigga I've ever met. Boss is a special type of man to keep my daughter's grave intact. Not to mention teach our son about his sister. It takes a real man to do some shit like that. Here I am trying to get over loving him and I'm reminded of why I love him so much. I hate Stone every day of life. From the grave, he's still finding a way to keep a bitch unhappy. Nevertheless, I'm blessed to be a free woman. There were many days I laid in my bunk and dreamed to be out in the land of the living, running my business, and taking care of my son. Now that I'm out here, I just don't know what to do with myself. I need to stop worrying about my past because it's hindering my future.

*****

I had been trying my best to cheer Shannie up, but she had been so depressed, especially since Kartier's daughter ended up having to live with them after all. Shannie had been trying her best to be brave in front of Kartier, but when she was alone, she would cry. Things had gotten so bad that she wasn't able to work through the day without having a breakdown. I felt so bad for my friend because I know how much she loves that nigga. So, finding out he has a daughter was a blow to her heart. I couldn't take her pain away, but I was doing everything in my power to be supportive. I owed her that much because she had been there for me in some of my darkest moments.

Since it was the weekend, I decided to book us spa appointments at Massage Envy and a room at the Westin on Michigan Ave. I was pulling out all of the stops to make sure my friend had a good time. Lord knows she needed a getaway from it all.

******

"Where the fuck you going, Shannie?" Kartier yelled. I was sitting on the couch, waiting for her so that we could leave. I had no idea this bitch was going and trying not to tell him. All of the kids were with Kartier and Boss' mother, Karen, so we were without a doubt about to take full advantage of our free weekend. It's not often she babysits because she loves to party and go to the boat.

As soon as we were walking out the door, he and Boss were walking in. I had never heard him raise his voice, ever. This nigga was in straight beast mode. He had me scared for my friend.

"I told you I'm having a ladies weekend with K'Yonnah. I need to get away from it all."

"What the fuck you mean get away from it all? I don't understand what the fuck that means, so enlighten me." Shannie sat on the couch and started scrolling through her phone. Before I knew it, Kartier walked over and snatched her phone from her hand. He walked towards the front door and launched that bitch. He slammed the door and snatched Shannie up by her shirt. That made me and Boss shoot up from where we were sitting.

"Calm down, bro."

"Don't tell me to calm down bro. She's trying to leave me. I can feel it. She has packed and everything. I'm not letting her take my family from me. I fucked up, ma. You just gone leave a nigga like that? No second chance or nothing." Kartier brought tears to my eyes standing there pouring his heart out. It was funny as hell too. He went from acting a fool to crying in a matter of seconds. That's a nigga for you. At the same time, it showed that he loved Shannie and their kids; he just made a mistake. I looked over at her and I could tell he had her about to cry too.

"I'm not leaving you, Kartier. I love you and our kids. It's just all been so much. K'Yonnah planned a weekend getaway just for us. That's all, bae."

"Come here, man. Stop crying." He pulled Shannie into his arms and they hugged each other.

"You two motherfuckers crazy! I'm out of here," Boss said and walked out the door, shaking his head. I couldn't help but laugh. Then a bright idea popped in my head.

"I can't go after all, Shannie. Why don't y'all go and spend the weekend together. It's all paid for. You guys need this getaway. In all my years of knowing you guys as a couple, I've never seen you like this. I love you both. Now go and enjoy yourselves."

"Are you sure, sis?" Kartier asked.

"I'm positive. Go make shit right with my girl."

"I'll make shit right, but I'll pay for us this weekend. You just rebook your weekend and save it for you guys to do something together. Thanks, Yonnah."

"You're welcome, bro. Love you, friend." I hugged Kartier and Shannie and headed out. I hopped in my car and found myself not really wanting to go home, so I decided to just go ahead and take advantage of the weekend getaway. It was in the heart of downtown, so I would take advantage and enjoy the sights.

About an hour after receiving my full body massage and getting a much-needed bikini wax, I checked into my hotel room. It was on the executive floor and it had a beautiful view of the Magnificent Mile. Downtown Chicago at night was so beautiful. I was bored as hell alone in my room, so I decided to go grab a bite to eat and a cocktail.

"Will that be all, ma'am?" the waitress asked.

"Yes, that's all. You can just bring the check." She nodded and walked away. I sat and sipped the rest of my Long Island Iced Tea, waiting for her to bring the check back. I looked up and instantly caught a major attitude. Boss was sitting about four booths over with some chick that looked plastic as fuck. I couldn't believe he was out with another bitch. True, he's married to someone else, but so fucking what. He ain't got no business entertaining another bitch. The attitude I had mixed with the Long Island had me in full petty mode. I placed a one-hundred-dollar bill on the table. I knew it would cover my meal and a tip for the waitress.

I grabbed my purse and walked right by the table where Boss was. I made sure to bump it hard as hell. I looked back and laughed because a glass of water fell on the bitch's dress that was sitting with him.

"Watch it, bitch, this is Givenchy! This fucking stain will never come out."

"I got your bitch!" I said as I started to walk back towards them.

"What the fuck is you on K'Yonnah?"

"Wait a minute. You know her, Boss?" The bitch was now standing with her hands on her hips.

"It's cool, CoCo. This is my son's mother. I'll handle it." Boss pushed me towards the entrance and I turned around and pushed him away from me.

"Don't put your fucking hands on me. What the fuck are you doing in there with some bitch?"

"First of all, calm the fuck down. Second, don't question what the fuck I do because I don't question you. Third, this is a fucking business meeting and if you don't want to get me or you murked, you would take your ass home. Right now!" he said through gritted teeth.

"What are you talking about, Karion?"

"Take your motherfucking ass home! You are not my wife, so you shouldn't be asking me any fucking questions anyway. Fuck outta here with this shit. You doing all of this for what? I thought you didn't love me. I thought you wanted space from me. Right now your actions are that of a bitter ass baby momma. The K'Yonnah I know is way too classy for the shit you just pulled. For the sake of our relationship as parents to our son, please walk away before I embarrass your ass out here." Never had Karion spoken to me in such a disrespectful manner. I snatched away from him and walked away from his ass. The whole walk back to my car I tried my best to hold back the tears that were threatening to fall. I was hurt because of the way he spoke to me and because he was telling the truth. I wasn't his wife, so I really shouldn't have behaved that way. I did tell him that I didn't love him and it was best we kept our distance from one another. The fact was, I still loved him and every time we had sex, it made me want him more and more. I had to tell him I no longer loved him and to stay away. Each time we fucked, he had to get up and go home to his wife. I know he's married, but the motherfucker doesn't have to keep reminding me. Once I made it to my car, my phone started to go off with a text notification. I knew it was Boss because of the ringtone. I reached over in the passenger seat and read the text from Boss.

Lil Boss Daddy: Where the fuck you going? I'm right behind you. I looked up in my rearview mirror and sure enough, he was behind me.

Me: Headed back to the Westin.

Lil Boss Daddy: Fuck you doing at the hotel. Let me find out.

Me: Ain't shit to find out. I'm chilling. I'm not your wife nigga. So don't ask me no fucking questions.

Lil Boss Daddy: You all in your fucking feelings huh? We'll see in a minute if you gone keep talking all that fly shit. What's your room number?

Me: Don't worry about what room I'm in. Take ya ass home to your wife.

Karion had me fucked up if he thought I was about to fuck with him after the way he talked to me. Fuck him.

Chapter 11- Boss

K'Yonnah had me fucked all the way up if she thought the shit she had just pulled was cool. That shit she did could have cost both of us our lives. The bitch she wasted the fucking water on is one of the biggest distributors of cocaine in the Midwest. I had finally gotten a meeting with her. The shit had been months in the making and in less than a minute, Yonnah might have fucked up my chance to get my bricks from her. I had recently parted ways with my old distributor because the shit he was selling was garbage. I had come too far to lose all of my fucking clientele, so it was best I part ways and go in a different direction.

CoCo could have given the word to have me and K'Yonnah murked. Unbeknownst to K'Yonnah and other patrons in the restaurant, her men were stationed throughout the restaurant and around the perimeter. That's why I snapped out on her ass. She knows motherfucking well I'm not about to be out with some random ass bitch. Then again, she doesn't know because she has no idea how deep I am in the drug game. She thinks that I'm a legit businessman. I do own several businesses that I run alongside my brother, but they're all fronts for our drug empire. I preferred for K'Yonnah not to know that part of my life. Mainly because she's so delicate to certain things in life. She's very naïve to street shit. Stone fucked her head up by never introducing her to the street life. Killing him and doing time in prison has her all fucked up, so I choose to deal with her differently. K'Yonnah is special and delicate like a flower. I never want to hurt her feelings or make her cry, but she has to understand that certain shit ain't cool. Like every time we fuck, she reminds me afterward that she doesn't love me or says that we can't keep having sex. As a man, I know it's wrong to make love to her and go home to Meesh, but I can't help the fact that I'm still in love with my baby momma and I can't bring myself to leave my wife. Meesh has held a nigga down and I would be less of a man to leave her now. Especially with her carrying my seed. In a way, I'm selfish to K'Yonnah and Meesh because I want them both. I'm in love with K'Yonnah and I love my wife. There's a big difference.

******

"So you just gone stand right here in the lobby and make a scene." K'Yonnah was sitting in the lobby of the hotel, refusing to go up to her room. She was being a real brat right now. It was actually turning me on so she better tighten up before I have them legs up in the air. We all know K'Yonnah be running from the dick.

"Yep. I'm going to sit right here because you're not going to my room. Take your ass home, Boss." I bit the inside of my jaw trying my best to calm down. I had never seen her be this slick at the mouth with a nigga. Had me feeling some type of way. Here I am trying to be all soft with her ass, but I see I have to take a different approach with her ass. It's obvious she has forgotten I'm that nigga the streets call Boss.

"Get your ass up and let's go now!" Before I knew it, I had yanked her ass up and pushed her towards the elevators. I was so done playing with her ass at the moment. She tried to walk fast, but I was right on her ass. After waiting a couple of minutes, the elevator came and I pushed her ass on there.

"Don't touch me!" she yelled as she pressed the number twelve. I remained calm and waited until the elevator got to the floor and let her lead the way to her room. As soon as she put the key card in and opened the door, I grabbed her by the back of the neck and pinned her ass to the wall.

"This what you want, K'Yonnah? You want me to give you some fucking attention, huh?" I bit down gently on the back of her neck and she shook her head from side to side.

"No, Karion. I don't want any attention. Just go, please," she said above a whisper.

"Your mouth telling me one thing, but your body language is telling me different. I bet your pussy wet as fuck right now." I slid my hand up her dress and snaked around to the front of her. To my surprise, she didn't have any panties on and that made my job much easier. I spread her legs apart so that I could play with that pussy. Her pussy was wet just like I thought. She moaned out in pleasure as I pinched her clit in between my fingers.

"Mmmmmmmm!" I roughly turned her around and made her look at me in my face. I needed to look in her eyes while I fucked her. I unzipped the slacks I was rocking and pulled my dick out of my Polo boxers. I grabbed her hand and glided it up and down my shaft. It swelled up instantly at her touch. I smiled devilishly as she bit her bottom lip seductively.

"Tell ya baby daddy you want the dick and I'll give it to you."

"I want that dick, Baby Daddy."

"That's all you had to say to begin with. You ain't got to act out and misbehave to get anything from me." I lifted her up and she wrapped her legs around my waist. We kissed passionately as I carried her over to the bed. For the rest of the night, I fucked her brains out and she showed me just how much she needed this dick in her life. K'Yonnah's pussy was so fucking good that after cumming back to back, a nigga fell asleep in the pussy. I woke up and the sun was shining through the drapes and she was asleep on my chest. I searched for my phone and found it on the floor. It was nine in the morning and there were numerous texts and calls from Meesh, Kartier, and my mother. I read them and my heart stopped. Meesh had gone into labor.

"Oh shit!" I jumped up, not meaning to knock K'Yonnah off of me.

"What's wrong?" she asked as she wiped her eyes.

"Meesh went into labor! Fuck! Fuck!" I can't believe I didn't hear my jack ringing. I looked at my phone and that's when I realized the ringer was off. K'Yonnah had this look on her face and it spoke volumes.

"Why, K'Yonnah?"

"I didn't want you to leave me. I love you too. I needed you here with me." She was now crying, but that shit didn't move me.

"Fuck outta here dawg! Man, that shit wasn't right. We're done, K'Yonnah. I'm not fucking with you no more. That was some snake ass shit to do. Why would you do something like that? It's not your fault that we fucked, but your selfishness caused me to possibly miss the birth of my daughter."

"I'm sorry, Boss!"

"Fuck you and your apology." I put on my shit and rushed to the hospital, leaving her ass bawling. She should be crying because that was some flaw ass shit she did.

******

"Where have you been, Karion Miller?" my mother said as she rushed towards me.

"Long story, Ma. Where's Meesh?"

"They getting ready to prep her for a C-Section. Get your ass back there. I'll talk to you afterward."

"I fucked up, bro," I said to Kartier as I walked towards the nurses' desk to let them know who I was.

"I already know where you were. It's not a coincidence neither of you answered the phone. Fuck all that, though. You're here now and that's all that matters. Go back there and see your daughter brought into the world," he said as he patted me on the shoulder.

"My wife, Meesha Miller, was brought in for labor and delivery. Can I go back there?"

"She'll be going up for surgery in a minute. Let me get you back there so that you can see your daughter being born." The nurse walked me to the back and Meesh was sitting up in bed with a blue surgical bonnet on her head. Her mother rolled her eyes at me in disgust.

"How nice of you to join us. I guess you can be in the delivery room with her. I'll be out in the waiting room." She kissed Meesh on the forehead and walked out, making sure to roll her eyes at me as she walked out of the room.

"Don't you dare come any closer to me. I don't want you touching me with her scent on you. That bitch's pussy that good that it would cause you to not answer the phone for me. I kept thinking this woman wanted to take you from me, but in reality, she already had you. The only thing that kept you with me was the fact that we got married and I was there to help raise your son. You never really loved me, Karion. I was just something to do while your baby momma was locked up. Silly of me to ever think that I was all you ever wanted and needed. In my heart, I've always known she was your first choice and I was her runner-up. I'm tired of competing with a woman I don't even compare to. You're in love with her and you love me. I can feel it in the way you touch me, talk to me, look at me, and make love to me. I'm officially done fighting for you. I want a divorce. All I ask is that you take care of my daughter and do your part as a father. Now get the fuck out. I don't want you in the delivery room with me and you just jumped out that bitch's pussy. They'll let you know when your daughter is here. Call my mother; I want her in the room with me." Before I could even respond, the transporter had arrived to take her upstairs. There was so much I wanted to say, but I could tell she had made her mind up. At the same time, what could I say in regards to this shit I have going on with K'Yonnah. Right now wasn't even the time to try and explain it. My main concern was Meesh giving birth to my daughter. As they wheeled her out of the room, I kneeled down and kissed her on the forehead.

"I love you, Meesh."

"I hate to admit it, but I love you too, Karion. More than you will ever know." As bad as I wanted to be in the delivery room, I had to respect Meesh's wishes. Her mother accompanied her back there and I headed back out to the waiting room. K'Yonnah was now sitting in the waiting area with the rest of the family. I couldn't even bring myself to look or sit by her ass. Her actions had me wanting to lay hands on her ass. That and the fact that she was holding our son on her lap.

"I'm so fucking disappointed in you, Karion."

"I'm sorry, Ma."

"I'm not the one who deserves an apology. Let's all bow our head in prayer that Meesh and the baby have a successful delivery." We all grabbed hands and my mother led us in prayer. My nerves were a wreck and I wouldn't be able to relax until she was out of surgery.

Four hours later

I watched as Meesh's mom came out and she didn't look too good. She came and sat down in silence. The doctor had a somber look on his face and that was a look I was familiar with. I just knew the baby didn't make it.

"Mr. Miller, we ran into some complications during the C-section. After we delivered the baby girl, your wife's heart stopped. Several attempts were made to resuscitate her, but we were unsuccessful. I'm sorry, but your wife didn't make it. As for your daughter, she was premature and her lungs are underdeveloped so we had to place her on a ventilator. If you would like to see her, she's in the NICU. Again, I'm sorry for your loss and we do have the hospital chaplain on call for you and your family." The sound of Meesh's mother screaming and my mother crying and praying wasn't enough to register what the doctor had just told me.

"Man, bro, I'm sorry," Kartier said as he sat next to me.

"Why is she here? My daughter is back there dead and his mistress is sitting here like she cares." Meesh's mother was now standing and hollering at K'Yonnah.

"Get K'Yonnah and Lil Boss out of here, bro. I don't want my son seeing all of this." Without a word, Shannie and K'Yonnah, along with the kids got up to leave the hospital.

"That's right, get the fuck out!" Meesh's sister, Mariah, yelled out.

"Watch that shit! We understand y'all hurt and upset, but watch your fucking mouth in front of the kids."

"I will never forgive you. You're the reason my daughter is back there dead," Meesh's mother said as she and the rest of their family left the hospital.

"This is not your fault, son. Don't let anybody blame this on you. This is all God's work and we won't question Him. Get yourself together so you can go see your daughter."

"How the fuck am I going to raise my daughter without her mother? I know I'm not supposed to question God, but why would He do this?" I put my head down and a nigga was in tears because this shit couldn't be life right now. Regardless of me cheating and fucking with K'Yonnah, it doesn't take away from the fact that I loved my wife. Some people might disagree, but I beg to differ. I loved my wife. I just wish she truly knew that before she left this world. I can't bring her back, but as long as I live, I'll keep her memory alive and my daughter will know how much her mother wanted her.

After sitting in the waiting room a little while longer, I got the courage to go and see my daughter. She was so damn tiny but beautiful as hell. I wanted to touch her, but I was just too afraid that I would hurt her.

"I promise Daddy is gone be here for you no matter what. I'm gone try my best to give you the world or die trying to give it to you." She moved around a little and that made me tear up because that let me know that she heard what her daddy was saying to her.

"Hey, Dad. Did you decide a name for yet?" the nurse asked.

"Miracle Meeshara Miller." She was indeed a Miracle and it was only right I give her her mother's name.

"That's beautiful. I'll be sure to take great care of Little Miss Miracle while she's here. I'm so sorry for your loss."

"Thank you." After sitting with my daughter for a little while longer, I signed some paperwork so that Meesh's body could be delivered to a funeral home the following day. I cried as I stood over her body. They had yet to take her down to the morgue, so she was still in the operating room with a sheet over her. I removed the sheet from her face just enough to kiss her. Her body was still warm.

"I'm so sorry for everything, ma. I promise to take care of our daughter and be there for her always." I sat in the chair in the room next to her until they came and took her down to the morgue. I had no idea how I was going to be able to look at my daughter without seeing Meesh. She was the spitting image of her mother. Life for me will never be the same after this shit. It's taught me one of the most valuable lessons, and that's to cherish every moment you have with people while they're here on this earth. As bad as I wanted to go home, I couldn't bear going to the house I shared with Meesh. Instead, I went to my OG's house and cut myself off from the world. At this point, I didn't have it in me to deal with anybody.

Chapter 12- K'Yonnah

It had been well over two weeks since I had last heard or seen Boss. From what Shannie told me, Boss was so distraught that he couldn't even make the arrangements. He allowed Meesh's mom to handle everything. Meesh never wanted a funeral, so they had a private closed casket memorial and she ended up being cremated. I wasn't able to pay my respects, but I did send flowers to the chapel. Her mother was being so ignorant that she didn't even allow Lil Boss or Ms. Miller to attend the services. That old lady was a different type of evil. Lil Boss had been having nightmares since all of this happened. I had been spending all of my time trying to soothe him and make him understand death. No matter what transpired between Meesh and me, she was still a mother to my son while I was away. My son was raised in a house with her for five years, so of course her passing affected him greatly. From the jump, I respected her as a mother to my son because she didn't have to raise him. The issue came in when she tried to come for me about her husband. That and the fact that Boss and I did have an affair. That's my only regret in all of this. I should have been stronger and not given in to temptation. I was dead ass wrong for the part I played in fucking with Boss. I love him and I'm not going to change that just because his wife is dead. I can, however, respect the fact that I'm the last person he wants to fuck with right now. What I can't respect is the fact that he has been neglecting our son. He's mourning and that's understandable, but Lil Boss needs him.

I've tried reaching out to him, but apparently he has blocked my number. All I want to do is explain my actions that night we were together. I cut his phone off before it even started to ring strictly because I knew that he would get up and leave. I never anticipated that something like that would happen. In a way, I was selfish because when he went to sleep, I should have woken him up so that he could go home, but I wanted him there with me. No matter my reason behind my actions, it still looks bad on my part. It looks as if I saw his wife calling and I silenced the ringer. That was not the case. I've gone above and beyond trying to apologize, but he's not trying to hear it. I refuse to keep trying, so the best thing would be to fall back and let him mourn in peace.

******

"So you haven't heard from him since that day?" Shannie asked me. We were eating lunch in my office and catching up with the latest.

"No. I've tried reaching out to him, but he's blocked my number. He hasn't seen Lil Boss since the services. I don't care what the fuck he does to me, but Lil Boss doesn't deserve to be ignored."

"I said I wasn't going to say anything, but Boss is all fucked up. He's drunk all the time and he hasn't been up to the hospital. He's too depressed to do anything. Ms. Miller has been up there around the clock taking care of the baby. Meesh's family talked all that shit and they haven't lifted a finger to care for that baby. Come to find out, Meesh had an insurance policy and made her mother and sister the beneficiary. Boss paid for everything out of his pocket. Those money hungry bitches cashed in those policies and ain't nobody heard from them." I just shook my head listening to that shit. That bitch did all that talking like her daughter was her biggest concern. Here it is her granddaughter is in the hospital and she couldn't care less.

"That's some sad shit. Boss needs to snap out of it because that baby needs his ass. I know I should keep my distance, but I think I'm going to go to the hospital and help out with the baby. Ms. Miller needs a break. Has Kartier tried talking to him?"

"Girl, yes, but they came to blows because Boss was drunk and talking crazy. Ms. Miller is going crazy trying to keep the peace with her sons, take care of Baby Miracle, and make sure Boss is okay." I sat in deep thought thinking about how bad things really were. As much as I wanted to give Boss his space, I knew right now I should probably just take the initiative and get on his ass. The Boss I know would never fold like this. At the same time, all I could do was think about how he was there for me when I lost my daughter. I would never have made it through without him, so it's only right I do the same for him.

"After work, I'm going to go over to Ms. Miller's house and take Lil Boss with me. Since he can't come see him, I'm taking Lil Boss to see him. That will be my way of getting close and talking some sense into him."

"You got my prayers. That nigga been on one lately. Let me get out of here. Kartier wants to take Paris to the doctor to get her checked out. Plus, she needs a physical to start school." I smiled at my friend because she had finally started to deal with having Paris in her house. Things with her and Kartier were better as well. She has that sparkle back in her eyes and I'm so happy for her.

After Shannie left, I finished some paperwork and headed over to pick Lil Boss up from baseball practice. He was adamant about joining Little League. That's another reason I'm so pissed off with Boss. Lil Boss really wants him to come and help him with his pitching and hitting. I was trying my best to explain to him why his father couldn't come and help him, but I was officially tired of making excuses for him. His ass was going to have to explain shit to his son himself.

*****

"Mommy, is my Daddy going to come to my first game?" I looked at my son in the rearview mirror as he went on and on about baseball.

"We'll ask him when we get over to grandma's house. Remember Daddy is very sad about Meesh so he might not be in the best of spirits. We need to try and cheer Daddy up."

"Okay, Momma. Is my baby sister here with him?"

"No, baby. She's still in the hospital for now. Her lungs aren't strong enough just yet for her to come home." Lil Boss asks a million questions about Miracle on a daily basis and I try my best to explain things to him. He's only six and very smart for his age.

When I pulled up to Ms. Miller's house, she was also getting out of her car. Before I could stop good, Lil Boss jumped out of the car and ran up to her. I smiled because I was so happy he had his grandmother in his life. I know that if my parents were alive, they would just eat him up.

"What did I tell you about jumping out of the car like that little boy?"

"Sorry, Ma. I missed my Glam-Ma."

"That's right he missed his Glam-Ma. Go inside the house and see your daddy. I need to talk to your momma real quick." Lil Boss ran in the house while me and her sat on the swing that was on her porch.

"What's going on, Ms. Miller?"

"Call me Lena. I hate that Ms. Miller shit." I couldn't help but laugh at her. She was in rare form today.

"I'm sorry, Lena."

"It must have been meant for you to come over because I was going to reach out and ask you to come over. Now you know I don't sugarcoat or condone shit, so I'll be the first to let you know that what you and Karion were doing was dead ass wrong. However, if there is nothing else I know as a woman; it's the heart wants who it wants and nothing else matters. I also know that my son is in love with you. Outside of me, you're the only one who can talk to him. Now I know that he's upset with you right now, but fuck all that. He's trying to find someone else to blame for his fuck up. I told that motherfucker straight up that he had no business at the hotel in the first place. Don't you let him blame this shit on you. I can look at you and tell that you feel guilty about Meesh passing. I can assure you it's not your fault or his. Meesh's body simply gave out from childbirth. The doctor told her that it was a possibility that something like that could happen. I was over at their house packing things up and I found a DNR paper. That girl had been informed on what could possibly go wrong and she still took that risk just to give Boss a baby. I understand her need to fulfill her dream of giving him a baby, but she did it for all the wrong reasons. At this point, that's neither here nor there. All I know is the baby is here and Boss needs to get the fuck out of this funk because it won't bring Meesh back. It's almost time for the baby to come home and he hasn't done anything. I really need you to talk some sense into him before I beat the shit out of him. I'm tired, K'Yonnah. I need a vacation from it all. My boyfriend booked me a flight to Vegas and

I'm out of here tomorrow. Please stay here and try to get a handle on things before I come back next week."

"I'll do what I can, Lena. Don't be surprised if you come back and I've killed his ass for fucking with me. This is not going to be easy and I know he will give me the blues."

"It will definitely be a challenge, but for some reason, I have faith in you to get the job done. Please don't kill my baby, K'Yonnah." We both laughed and headed inside to go see Boss. When I walked inside, I turned my nose up in disgust at his ass. There was a pint of Patron and blunts all rolled up on the coffee table. I couldn't believe he was drinking and smoking weed as if our son wasn't sitting on the couch next to him. His mother just shook her head and walked to the back of the house.

"Baby, go in the back with your granny for a minute. Let me talk to your father." I waited until Lil Boss was all the way in the back before I snatched the Patron off the table and poured the shit out in the sink. I walked back over to the living room and grabbed all of the blunts and broke them bitches up into little pieces. Boss was staring at me with the death look and I knew he wanted to hit me, but I dared him to. He stood up quickly and we were face to face in a standoff.

"Your ass real lucky I would never put my hands on you, but you seriously trying to get knocked the fuck out. Coming over here fucking with me. I blocked your ass and now you over here. What part of I'm not fucking with you don't you understand, K'Yonnah?"

"Let's get some shit straight. I'm not here for me, I'm here because you need to get out of this funk and tend to your fucking kids. Especially Miracle. She's been in that hospital since her mother passed and you haven't been up there. Your ass is being real selfish to her right now. The Boss I know is a wonderful father and would never abandon his responsibilities. The Boss I fell in love with would go above and beyond to make sure his family was straight. Meesh is dead and she's not coming back. Miracle is alive and she needs her father to man the fuck up and take care of her. I don't care how you treat me, but you will not ignore my fucking son. Miracle is not my daughter, but I won't allow you to ignore her either. Meesh helped with Lil Boss and it's only right I help with Miracle. Get your shit together, nigga, and do the shit immediately. Your son has his first baseball game next week. He needs help with his pitching and hitting. You clean yourself up while I go shopping and get stuff for Miracle to come home." He stared at me the entire time I talked without so much as a word.

"You standing here all high and mighty talking about me and what the fuck I'm doing as a father, but let's talk about the fact that you did some sneaky shit and you're feeling guilty about it. That's why you're here trying to redeem yourself. As far as I'm concerned, you can get the fuck gone. I don't need you to do shit for my daughter. I got her and my son too. Fuck outta here, K'Yonnah!"

"Let's get some shit straight, nigga. I admit I cut your phone off, but I did it before your wife started to call you. I admit I should have woken you up when you went to sleep, but at that point, I wanted you there with me. At the same time, I told your ass to leave; it was you who insisted on coming up to my room. Stop sitting around trying to blame me for what the hell happened. I will not stand here and act as if I regret having sex with you because I don't. I'm not a fake ass bitch and I own up to my mistakes, unlike your ass, who's sitting around sulking over some shit you had no control over. Do you actually think Meesh would want you to be like this? I don't think so. Now you can feel whatever fucking way you want to feel about me because I can't change that. However, like I said before, you will get your shit together and be the father these kids need you to be." I grabbed my purse and got the fuck out of there. I made sure to leave Lil Boss behind in hopes that it would help his father out of this funk. The way Boss spoke to me didn't hurt because I know he's really hurt himself. Being the woman that I am, I intended on keeping my word on doing what I could for Miracle. I went to Target and picked up all of the things she would need for when she came home. As I walked around the store, a part of me felt as if I had been too hard on Boss. I knew that he was mourning and beating himself up about everything. His hurt made him lash out at me. I wasn't making excuses for him. It's just that the Boss that I'm in love with takes over the Boss that's losing his damn mind right now. I wanted to remain mad at him, but my heart wouldn't allow me to. After I finished shopping, I headed home to relax and clear my mind. When I pulled into my driveway, I was surprised to see Boss' truck in the driveway. I had given him a key when I first moved in in case of an emergency.

I grabbed what bags I could from the trunk and headed inside. I smiled seeing him and our son on the couch playing *Call of Duty: Modern Warfare*. I hated for him to play that game, but right now, I welcomed it. My baby missed his daddy so any type of quality time was good enough for me.

I placed the bags of clothes and other items on the dining room table and headed to the kitchen to find something to cook. As I looked in the fridge, I realized I had nothing quick to eat and all of the meats were frozen solid. I would be all night trying to cook. Instead, I decided to order some pizza, hot wings, and chicken alfredo.

"I ordered some food for you guys. Listen for the delivery man. It's already paid for."

"Come in here with us, Momma."

"No, baby. You go ahead and play with your daddy. I'll be upstairs taking a nap. I'm so tired." I kissed my son on the forehead and headed to my bedroom. Boss and I had yet to say anything to one another and that was fine with me. Just seeing him shaved, looking clean, and smelling good was more than enough for me. I smiled as I laid across the bed because I knew I had gotten to Boss and that made him get off his ass. That was a good start.

Chapter 13- Boss

I stood in the doorway of K'Yonnah's bedroom, watching her sleep. She looked just like the angel she was. I looked at her and I couldn't help but feel fucked up for how I've treated her. From the jump, I've always known that she loved a nigga. Just like I've always loved her. When she went away, I felt like it was the end of whatever we had. Technically, we never got a chance to get in a relationship. It's like she came home and Meesh was here, but she wasn't. Not to be misconstrued because I did love Meesh; it's just that I loved K'Yonnah more. I made a vow before God, so there was no way I could just leave my wife. I was obligated to her. No matter what transpired between K'Yonnah and me, I would never want Meesh dead. Her death had fucked me up in the head. I think the thing that fucked me up the most was the fact that I wasn't there when she needed me the most. Shit just went blank for me when she died. Guilt will make you lose your fucking mind. I now know what the fuck depression feels like. It had me so fucked up that I couldn't even bring myself to go and see my fucking daughter. I'm a thorough ass nigga and my actions with my children had me looking weak ass fuck. My mother, Kartier, and even Shannie had been trying to get me out of my funk, but I wasn't budging. It's funny how the one person I was trying to block from my life had the power to give me back the life I so needed. I'll ask for God's forgiveness for all the days of my life, but I'm not sorry for loving K'Yonnah. Truthfully, I missed the fuck out of her and I hadn't had a good night's sleep since that night I spent with her. I knew for a fact she wasn't fucking with me, but I needed her to make me better. I removed my shoes and climbed into bed with her. She was so out of it that she didn't even feel me in bed with her. I laid my head on her chest and drifted off to sleep, not caring if she would wake up and curse me out. Right about now, she was feeling like the softest place on Earth.

****

The next morning, I woke up in K'Yonnah's bed in nothing but my boxers and underneath the covers. I looked over and K'Yonnah was no longer in bed. The smell of food cooking permeated the air and my stomach began to growl. I could go for some food because I had basically been living off of Tequila and Kush. Just the thought of the shit made me sick to my stomach.

I sat up in bed and sitting at the foot was a new toothbrush and some clean clothes. That piqued my interest because I didn't even bring clothes with me. After I showered, I walked through the house to find K'Yonnah.

"Good morning," she said as she stood in the kitchen in a pair of leggings and a sports bra.

"Good morning, ma. Where's Lil Boss?"

"He had practice this morning. I didn't wake you up because I knew you were tired. Sit down so you can eat." I sat down and K'Yonnah placed a plate of cheese eggs, grits, and a T-bone steak. I went straight in for the kill. K'Yonnah fixed her a plate of food and joined me at the table. We sat in silence as we devoured the food. After the silence became awkward, I decided to try and break the ice.

"Thanks, ma. I can't remember the last time I ate. As a matter of fact, this is your first time cooking for me. I always wondered if your ass could cook."

"Well, I can cook. Since you'll be here for a while, you'll get to see my skills. While you were asleep, I went over to your mom's house and got your belongings. She's gone to Vegas with her boyfriend. I didn't want you to be over there by yourself. You need to be around people that love you. Plus, Miracle gets to come home in a couple of days. We need to get the house in order for her arrival. This house is huge so there's more than enough room for you guys.

Now before you get all upset about me not speaking to you first, I did what I thought was best for all of us. Your daughter needs a stable environment and your son misses you. As for me, I need you here so that I can take care of you just like you did when I was in a fucked up situation. You went above and beyond to make sure that I was okay even when I was still in love with a man who whooped my ass. I don't take it to heart the things you said because I know you didn't mean it. Let's just start fresh and focus on what's important and that's the kids. Now hurry up and eat. We have to get to the hospital and visit with Miracle."

"Yes, ma'am. I guess your name should be Boss instead of mine."

"You the Boss, baby. I'm just being the Lady you need me to be." She winked her eye at me and placed her plate in the sink. I couldn't even argue with K'Yonnah if I wanted to. After all, I really did need some help with Miracle. I'm not going to even front; when I laid in bed with K'Yonnah last night, the shit felt like home. For some reason, I felt like with K'Yonnah is where I needed to be. Not because Meesh was now deceased, but because with K'Yonnah is where I've belonged all along. When she went away, I needed something to fill the void and it came in the form of another woman. I can't say it enough how much I did love Meesh, she just wasn't K'Yonnah. No matter how I tried to force myself to do the right thing by my wife, my heart and soul were with K'Yonnah.

Just sitting here and listening to her tell me the way things were going to be had me feeling better about the situation already. As I watched her move around the kitchen, cleaning and putting away the dishes, I became entranced. I quickly got up and walked behind her.

"I'm sorry for blaming you. Nothing that happened was your fault. My selfish need to want you while I was still married was wrong. I knew how you felt about what we were doing. I knew that you were genuine when you said that you didn't want to be a home wrecker. It was just so hard for me to be in your presence and not want to make love to you. When you went away, I was fucked up in the head because I wanted you but I couldn't have you. I felt like we never had the chance to be what we were destined to be. I lost faith in us and I made the choice to move on. It was the only way I could get over you. I thought all of those feelings were gone but when you showed up at my house when you got out, all of those feelings came right back and I couldn't control them. Funny thing about it though was that I didn't want to control them. I wanted you and I needed you like air. It's like everything is happening around us for a reason. I think it's safe to say that this is our chance to finally be the couple that we never got a chance to be. Let's make this shit right, ma." I turned K'Yonnah around so that I could look into her eyes. Her face was drenched with tears. I pulled her in close and placed soft kisses on her forehead.

"Promise me that you won't ever hurt me. I need you to promise me that. All I know is pain and hurt from a man. I need you to love me like I need to be loved. You already know how to make love to my body. I'm not the same K'Yonnah I was when we first met. I need you to make love to my soul and to my mind because I don't know what that feels like these days."

"I promise to never hurt you and fulfill all your needs on every level. Tell me that you're going to be my Lady." I firmly gripped her ass and lifted her up on the sink.

"I've always been your Lady," she said as she grabbed my face and kissed me passionately. It seemed like the biggest weight in the world had been lifted off of my shoulder with that kiss. It solidified our bond, our strength, and our future. I had a second chance to be with the love of my life and God willing, I was going to give her the world.

"Come on and get dressed. I have something I want you to see."

About Two Hours Later

"Whose house is this? It's huge." K'Yonnah was standing in the driveway of a home I had built for her from the ground up.

"I bought this place about five years ago, right after I met you. I intended on showing it to you when we came back from New York, but Kartier had got hit up. Before I got a chance to show you, you had been arrested for killing Stone. I felt so bad because this was supposed to be a place of peace for you. I was going to kill Stone myself and bring you here to live. I've always beat myself up for not moving in on his ass quicker. All of this shit would have ended differently for us."

I placed the key inside the door and we walked in holding hands. I leaned back against the wall and marveled in the glow on K'Yonnah's face. It made a nigga feel good to see her smile. This moment should be frozen in time because I thought that I would never see this day. Now that it's here, I can't believe it.

"This house is just too much, Karion. I want you to know that you don't have to buy me lavish things. I can't miss anything that I've never had. I love you for you, not your money."

"Let's get something straight right now, K'Yonnah. Don't ever tell me what to do with my money. Especially when it comes down to you. You deserve to be spoiled and live lavishly. I want to give you the lavish life not because you've never had it, but because you deserve it. So, when are you going furniture shopping? I want us to all be moved in before the end of the month. Spare no expense on what you want. Don't ask me any questions. What you heart desires, you get it. Here, never leave home without this." I handed her my black card and walked out of the house. K'Yonnah was looking at me like I was crazy, but I was dead ass serious. She's not used to the life I lead, so it was important that I get her accustomed to the finer things in life, whether she wanted to or not.

Chapter 14- K'Yonnah

It had been a month since Boss and I made things official. Life for us had been going great and I couldn't ask for a better relationship with him. Gone were the guilty thoughts that plagued my mind about Meesh's death. I had been giving all of my energy into taking care of Boss and the kids. Miracle had finally gotten adjusted to being home from the hospital and sleeping through the night. At first, I was so scared to hold her because she was so tiny. That added with the fact that I didn't know the first thing about taking care of a baby. I missed out on everything with my son, so I've been more than happy to take care of the baby.

Boss is gone the majority of the time, out running his business. Since I have a daycare inside of my organization, Miracle gets to go to work with me every day and I check on her every hour on the hour. Lil Boss is doing better on his baseball team and in school. It seems as though things have been going great for our little family. I still have to pinch myself sometimes to make sure that I'm not dreaming. There were so many nights I dreamed about going to sleep lying next to Boss and waking up next to him in the morning. Now that I have everything I've dreamed of, I don't know what to do with it. Thank God, Boss has been patient with me adapting to his lifestyle because I've had the hardest time. I love that man more now than ever.

******

"How long will you be gone?" I asked Boss as he walked around our bedroom, packing for a business trip. I hated to pout and sound like a brat, but I didn't want him to go.

"Only for the weekend, bae. I'll be back home Monday night. I promise to call you every chance I get. This meeting is very important for Kartier and me. We've been working hard on this business deal."

"I know you guys have. I'm sorry. It's just that I feel like I'm going to cry if you leave." I quickly wiped my eyes because tears had welled up and threatened to fall.

"Seriously, Yonnah, are you crying right now?" He laughed.

"Don't laugh at me, Karion. It's not my fault that I'm used to you being here with us. How in the hell am I going to sleep at night without you?"

"Awww, look at my big baby. You got me about to cry, ma. I tell you what. I'll Facetime you every night and we can talk until you fall asleep. Don't think for a minute I'm not going to miss you and the kids, but I have to go. If I don't work, we don't eat, ma. Now give Daddy a kiss with ya spoiled ass." He pulled me closer to him and tongued me down like he was on his way to prison instead of a business trip.

"I love you so much, Karion."

"I love you more, ma. Keep that pussy tight for me." He smacked me on the ass and grabbed his luggage to leave.

"Tell Daddy bye-bye, Miracle." I lifted her up so that he could kiss her on the forehead.

"See you later, Daddy's Princess. I'm going to stop by Lil Boss' school and see him before I head to the airport. Call me, Yonnah, if you need me. No matter what I'm doing, I'll answer my phone."

"I'll try not to call unless it's very necessary. Good luck on your business deal." We kissed one last time before he left out of the door. I watched him as he pulled out of the driveway. Despite me not wanting him to leave, in a way, I was elated at the moment. With everything that had been going on, I didn't even realize I had missed my period for two months. I had bought several pregnancy tests and I couldn't take them while he was in the house with me. My nerves were all frazzled.

I laid Miracle in her crib and cut her mobile on. I headed to the bathroom and opened all of the pregnancy tests. I bought four different brands just to see what the outcome would be. I peed on each test and set them on the sink. I sat biting my nails and scrolling through my phone for five minutes before I got the courage to look and I exhaled a sigh of relief. They were all negative. I was thanking my lucky stars. It wasn't that I didn't want another baby with Boss, it's just that I didn't have time for a baby at the moment. My organization was thriving and required more of my time. Not to mention the fact that we have a newborn baby that needs around the clock care. Let's not forget Boss doesn't have the time either. These days he's so engrossed in his businesses. The last thing I want to have is a house full of kids and have to hire a nanny to raise them. I refuse to have some strange ass woman in my house watching my children or around my man. That movie *The Hand That Rocks the Cradle* scared me straight.

Chapter 15- Shannie

Things between Kartier and I have been going great. Since the incident with Nikkita, it seems as though our relationship has gotten stronger. At first, the hardest thing in the world was adapting to her being in our household, but now I love her being in the house with us. Her brother and sister love her being there with them. At first, I thought it was going to be hard on them, but they adjusted quite well. Paris is a sweet little girl and I'm happy that she's with us because for some reason, I feel like there was more going on than just that nigga whooping on her and Nikkita. After a couple of weeks of being with us, she finally adjusted to not jumping when someone walked in the room. She also had a bad habit of locking all the doors at night. Especially her room.

Both Kartier and I had a long talk with her and told her that she was safe. We also had a long talk about if she had ever been touched inappropriately. She was adamant in the fact that she hadn't, but I still have a funny feeling that she was. When we took her to the doctor, she got a good report. Her hymen was still intact and that made both Kartier and me feel better about the situation. I was more elated than Kartier was because I knew if something had happened to her, he was going to go to prison for the rest of his life. He was going to kill Nikkita and that nigga, without a doubt.

K'Yonnah had the day off, so I was in the office making sure things were running smoothly. We both had so many other things going on that we were holding interviews for house staff to help with housekeeping and other household duties that would keep the center running smoothly in our absence.

"Excuse me, Shannie. There's a woman at the front desk who needs some assistance," my assistant Brionna said.

"Okay. Have her fill out the necessary forms and send her to the back."

"I already did. Here they are." She handed me the paperwork and walked out of the door. I looked over the paperwork, but quickly stopped when I heard a knock at the door.

"Hey, Shannie." This bitch had to be kidding me right now. It was Nikkita, and she looked fucked up. Her eyes were black and blue. The whites of her eyes were bloodshot red. I took a closer look and she had handprints on her face and neck. Not to mention, her swollen busted and bruised lips.

"Oh my God!" I said as I jumped up and rushed to close my office door. I grabbed her hand and she was shaking like a leaf.

"I didn't have anywhere else to go. My mom won't allow me to come to her house. Please, Shannie. I need your help. Promise me that you won't tell Kartier that I'm here." I looked at this bitch like she was crazy. One thing I didn't do was lie to my husband. If he found out I was hiding Nikkita out, he would have me looking like her ass looks now. Plus, he wants no parts of her ass after she chose that nigga over Paris.

"I'm sorry, Nikkita. Kartier will kill me if I don't tell him. Plus, you don't want any help. As soon as that nigga pops up you're going to go right with him. This center is a safe haven and I cannot compromise the other girls who are here in secret and choose to leave their abusive spouses. It's my job to advocate, but you have to be dedicated to walking away from this man."

"I'm done with him and I can assure you he will never bother me and my daughter again."

"What do you mean by that?"

"I killed that motherfucker. That's why I need your help. If I don't get rid of his body, I'm going to go to jail!" Nikkita began to cry and freak out. I sat down in my chair and tried to figure out what to do next.

"Where is his body, Nikkita?"

"It's in the trunk of my car."

"Wait a minute. You've been driving around with a dead body in your trunk?" I was now pacing back and forth, trying to gather my thoughts.

"I killed him in Texas and I drove back here with his body in the trunk." I grabbed my phone and I sent a text to K'Yonnah, telling her to get here immediately. Lord, I had no idea what I was going to do.

"I can't believe you did this, Nikkita. Do you have any idea how serious this is? You can go to jail for this. I know you don't want to, but we have to tell Kartier. Him and Boss can help us."

"Nooooo! We can't tell him. He's going to kill me for letting him hurt Paris. That's why I killed him. While he was beating me, he confessed to doing things to Paris. It's so foul I can't even bring myself to say it. After he beat me, he made me cook him dinner. I squirted a whole bottle of Visine in the food and mixed Promethazine in his Kool-Aid. I waited until he was out of it and fell asleep. I grabbed a steel bat and beat him until he was dead. I placed his body in the trunk and then I set the house on fire. That was two days ago. I had to kill him, Shannie. Death was the only way I could ensure that he wouldn't hurt me or my daughter again." I walked over to her and hugged her tight. I've seen so many women come through these doors trying to protect their daughters from men like him.

"I'm sorry this happened to you and Paris."

"What's going on, Shannie? Who is this?" K'Yonnah asked as she quickly walked into the office and closed the door behind her.

"This is Nikkita, Paris' mother. She has a big problem and now it's my problem because she just came in here and made me an accessory after the fact."

"Oh my God! What did y'all do?" she asked with her hands on her hips.

"I didn't do anything, but she killed her husband for abusing her and sexually abusing Paris."

"Wait a minute. I thought you said that the doctor confirmed that she had never been sexually assaulted."

"He did other things to her. Please don't make me repeat it." Nikkita cried on my shoulder. K'Yonnah looked at me with narrow eyes before speaking again.

"Look, this is serious. It's obvious that you're an abused woman. Did you ever report this to the police?" Nikkita shook her head no and that made K'Yonnah look worried. We locked eyes and I knew that we were both thinking the same thing.

"We have to come up with a foolproof plan to keep you out of jail. Now where is his body?"

"In my trunk."

"Come again."

"I killed him in Texas and I drove his body all the way here in my trunk. I couldn't risk his body being found in Texas. He's feared out there and no one would dare touch him. I would be the first person they looked at. No one gives a fuck about him out here. This was my only solution. I'll pay you guys whatever I can to help me bury his body out in the Forest Preserve."

"I think we need to call Kartier." I grabbed my phone and K'Yonnah snatched it from my hand.

"No! We can't do that. Him and Boss are on an important business trip and they can't be interrupted for something we can handle. We'll help you get rid of the body. I've been in your shoes before and I know what it feels like to sit in prison for killing a motherfucker that hurt you and your daughter. You don't have to pay us anything. However, you can make a donation to help other women who are in prison for murdering their abusive spouses. Not many of them are coming home. Right here and now we have to make a pact that we won't tell Boss or Kartier." K'Yonnah held her hand out and we followed by placing our hands one on top of the other. I couldn't believe I was getting ready to help my husband's baby's mother bury her damn husband. This some shit straight out of those damn urban fiction books K'Yonnah have my ass reading.

Chapter 16- Nikkita

I was trying my best not to cry as we rode to the Forest Preserve to bury

Cord. All I could think about was all the bullshit he had put me through during our four-year marriage. Cord was truly a devil disguised as an angel. It was as if he appeared out of the clear blue sky and made my life better. He came into my life when I was down and out. I was about to be evicted from my apartment when he walked into the management office in my housing complex and paid my rent in full for six months. I was so embarrassed standing there begging for an extension from the property manager. Had I not had my daughter and wasn't afraid to live on the streets with her, I never would have allowed him to do such a thing. Deep down inside, I knew that shit was too good to be true.

I had never seen Cord before that day and I had lived in the complex for well over a year. Afterward, we talked and I found out that he was actually a tenant in the complex. He told me that he had been watching and scoping me out for the longest. From that moment, we started up a relationship that ended up in a shotgun marriage a week later. Every day I beat myself up for not thinking things through. My stupid ass knows better than to do some shit like that. From the moment my mother found out what I had done, she didn't want anything to do with me. My gut told me that things weren't going to be all peaches and crème, but I went with the flow. I was in dire need and Cord was so good to me. He went above and beyond to show me that he wanted to be a father to my daughter. It was actually easy for me to fall for him because that's all I ever wanted for Paris.

I hate that I allowed my pride to get in the way and didn't reach out to Kartier sooner. There was never any bad blood between us. We fucked around, I got pregnant and we simply stopped fucking with each other. One thing I've never been and never will be is a bitter ass baby momma. I laugh at bitches who sit up and go above and beyond to hurt a nigga because he won't take care of his responsibilities. Fuck all that. I refuse to invest energy into foolishness. I would struggle before I'm out in the streets holding grudges against any man. At the same time, had I been more diligent with Kartier and upfront with Shannie sooner, I might not be in this predicament. Fuck it, though. I have no regrets about what I did to his ass. It's one thing for him to beat my ass, but a totally different thing for him to abuse my daughter. I hope his ass burns in hell.

About an hour later, we arrived at the Forest Preserve and I was more than ready to get rid of Cord's body. He was starting to rot and that smell was horrendous. We all had to wear face masks in an attempt to not inhale the stench, but the shit was so strong it really wasn't working. We drove around looking for the perfect spot.

"Right here is perfect. It's off the beaten path so no one will even think to come back here," K'Yonnah said as she pulled over and we all got out.

"How in the fuck did you put his big ass in this trunk?" Shannie asked as we struggled to carry his body out of the trunk.

"A wheelbarrow, and I damn near broke my back trying to get his ass in it." We dropped his body on the ground with a loud ass thud that caused us all to jump.

"Come on, let's get to digging. I have to get home in time for Boss to call."

"Same here. If Kartier calls and I'm not home, he's going to ask a million questions. My nerves so damn bad I might fuck around and spill the beans. I need to hurry up and get home so I can relax."

"Your ass needs to go smoke a blunt before you get us all knocked." We couldn't help but laugh because Shannie was without a doubt going to get us booked. She was nervous as hell. About four hours later, we had finally buried his body and headed back to the city.

"I just want to say thank you, ladies, for everything. I promise I owe my life to the both of you. Especially you, Shannie. Thank you so much for taking care of my daughter. As much as I want her with me right now, I know that it's not the right time. Plus, Kartier is not going to allow that after I left with Cord. Quiet as it's kept, I don't even know where I'm going to live at this point. I need to give my mother some time to get out of her feelings. She's pissed at me for going back to him. My momma can hold a damn grudge, so it's a wrap for me at the moment."

"You can stay at the center for as long as you like. No one will know that you're there. After about a month, things should be fine. Plus, you can get counseling for the trauma that you've been through. Just because Cord is dead and buried doesn't mean it's over; the nightmares have just begun. Trust me, sleep won't come easy for a while," K'Yonnah said.

"Thank you so much. I promise I'll repay you guys for everything. I know that this is only the beginning for my long road of mental recovery. I just want to get back on track so that I can be the mother Paris needs me to be." As I sat in the backseat, I asked God to forgive me for my sins. I begged Him to have mercy on my soul. The last thing in this life that I wanted to do was risk my chances of getting in the pearly gates. Hopefully, God will understand why I took His will into my own hands. My phone began to ring and I quickly looked at the screen to see who it was. I rolled my eyes because it was Cord's mother. I cut the phone off and made sure to break it into a million pieces. That bitch was evil as well and I wanted no parts of her. Cord was a momma's boy and she was madly in love with him like he was her damn man. That shit was so unhealthy to me. That's probably why he had no problem touching my daughter. Something was definitely fishy about Cord and his fat ass mama. At this point, that's neither here nor there. They're both a distant memory that will eventually fade.

Chapter 17- Boss

I had only been gone for two days and I was more than ready to get home to my family. I missed K'Yonnah and the kids like crazy. I didn't realize how much I missed them until I couldn't sleep without feeling their presence. Things were finally coming together for a nigga the way I had planned. Kartier and I had been busting our asses over the years to solidify ourselves in the drug game and for years, we've been doing just that. Having Coco LaRue as our connect would have us exactly where we need to be and that's right at the motherfucking top. I had a good feeling that she was going to agree to the terms that I intended to lay out for her.

I was growing restless waiting for her to call Kartier and me for the meeting that she called us down to Mexico for. It was as if she had us waiting on standby purposely. My patience was wearing thin, but I knew that I had to keep cool. The ball was in her court and we had to play by her rules if we wanted her to agree to give us the one hundred bricks.

"Do you think she's going to fuck with us?" Kartier asked.

"Hell, I don't know. We've talked several times since the incident where K'Yonnah made the wine fall on her. She told me shit was cool. I guess it really is since she invited us down for this damn last minute meeting. Her ass needs to hurry up because I'm ready to get home to my baby."

"Yonnah got you sprung as hell, my nigga." He laughed as he took a long pull off of the Kush blunt he was smoking.

"Don't do me nigga. Just a couple of months ago your ass was crying and begging like Keith Sweat when you thought Shannie was about to dip on your ass. Now that shit was funny as hell. At the same time, I feel you, though. I don't want to lose

K'Yonnah. That's why I'm debating on whether or not to tell her about my lifestyle. I think she has an idea about but chooses to play like she doesn't know what's going on. I never want there to be secrets between us."

"You have to tell her. We as men always take away a woman's right to choose what she wants. That's what I did to Shannie by not telling her about my daughter from the jump. Seeing the hurt in her eyes fucked me completely up. I'm glad that we're back on the right track, but she looks at me with untrusting eyes. It's like she always thinks I'm lying about shit, but never comes out and says anything. That's not a good way to live, lil bro. My advice would be to tell her. K'Yonnah loves you, so I know whatever you're with, she's with." At that moment, I knew that I was going to come clean with K'Yonnah. I can't risk losing her when I just got her after all of these years. K'Yonnah has me feeling like I want to pop the question. My baby deserves a ring and the wedding of her dreams. She's been going so hard for me and the kids. I wouldn't have it any other way. Now all I need to do is get this damn deal solidified so I can take my ass home and make love to my future wife.

*****

"I'm so happy you called us down, CoCo. For a minute, I was thinking that you weren't going to fuck with us," I said as Kartier and I walked inside of her lavish estate, which sat on the outskirts of Cancun, Mexico. Her security led us out to her huge backyard where she was lounging by the pool. I looked around and observed the many men she had stationed around her with AR-15s. They were itching for a motherfucker to get on bullshit so they could air their asses out.

"It's my pleasure, Boss. Why wouldn't I fuck with you two handsome brothers? Not only are you both two of the wealthiest kingpins in the drug game, you're also very low-key in the drug game. Not too flashy and you don't live overly extravagant. That's the main reason I'm going to be your distributor. I love to do business with men who think with their minds and not with their money. You're the type of business men I need to keep my organization thriving. So often organizations are dismantled by the Feds due to careless spending and extravagant lifestyles that scream I'm a dope dealer. As for me, I was born into legit wealth. The drug empire I've built is merely an extra source of income." CoCo Larue stood up and seductively adjusted her white and gold two-piece swimsuit that had crept in her fat ass. Coco was a bad bitch in every sense of the word. Beautiful, but very deadly. She was the type of bitch that would kill your family without so much as a blink of an eye. She winked at us and jumped in the pool and started to do laps.

"Man, it's time to get the fuck out of here," Kartier said under his breath.

"Hell yeah," I agreed. She needed to give us what we came for. All this extra shit she can keep. I don't give a fuck how sexy or how fat her ass is; she doesn't do shit for me. K'Yonnah is more than enough. Not to brag on my baby, but her ass is much fatter. Plus, I never mix business with pleasure. After about five minutes of watching her do laps around the pool, she was assisted out by one her maids. She walked towards us, dripping wet, without a care in the world.

"Let's talk business. Every first of the month you will receive one hundred bricks. Every fifteenth of the month, I expect to receive my cut. No excuses.

Max, get the Yayo! I have a jet waiting to take you back to the States. It was nice doing business with you gentleman. I'll see you on the fifteenth. Feel free to call me Karion if there is anything you need." She blew me a kiss and walked away with her security team.

"That bitch want to suck your dick my nigga."

"I'm straight. This dick belong to Yonnah. That bitch just blessed us with this merch. All I'm on is making sure she get her bread on time. Anything else she want from a nigga is a no go. I'll never mix business with pleasure." An hour later, we were on her jet with the bricks, headed back to the States. I rubbed my hands like Birdman all the way home in deep thought about how my brother and I were about to take this shit to another level.

*****

My eyes fluttered open as I woke up to the superb feeling of K'Yonnah giving me head. I was surprised because that was something she never did and I never really asked her to. Just the fact that she was waking a nigga up with this bomb ass head had me mad at myself for not getting it from her on a regular. She was giving a nigga that sloppy ass head too. I had to bite my bottom lip to keep from screaming like a bitch as she sucked sensually on the tip. She hooked her arms under my legs and damn near lifted my shit up in the air like I was a bitch. She swallowed my dick whole and was gagging like crazy. That made her mouth wetter and made me nut faster. I had never had a bitch suck my dick the way K'Yonnah was doing it. I damn near had a seizure as she licked in between my balls. She took her time as she sucked on each one gently. I had to start grabbing her hair and pushing her damn head away. I knew at any minute I was going to explode.

"Get back, ma." As soon as I shot my load in her mouth, she removed my dick and spit it out on the tip and licked all over it. She then proceeded to smack my dick across her face a couple of times before inserting it back in her mouth. I rocked up instantly. She raised up and sat down on my dick with ease and precision. I grabbed her titties as she began to rock back and forth slowly. I pulled her down so that I could suck on her nipples that looked like Hershey Kisses.

"Ohhhh babyyyy! I missed this dick so much."

"I missed that pussy too, ma. Turn around and ride that dick backwards. I want to see that pretty ass bouncing." My toes began to curl as K'Yonnah bounced up and down on my dick hard as hell.

"Like that, Daddy!" she said in a submissive tone.

"Just like that!" I said as I smacked her on both of her ass cheeks.

"Ohhhh fuckkk! I'm about to cum, Daddyyyy!"

"I don't want you to cum on that dick. Come up here and feed me. A nigga hungry as fuck!" K'Yonnah hopped up and walked to the head of the bed. She squatted on my face and I let her ride my face. I made sure to dart my tongue in and out of her pussy while my nose rubbed that clit."

"Oh my God, Karion! I'm cumming, bae! Ahhhhhhh!" K'Yonnah was releasing her juices all in my mouth and my face. I quickly flipped her over on her back and rammed my dick inside of her. I pushed her legs so far back that they were touching the wall above the headboard. She reached up and grabbed my face so that she could taste her juices.

"Fuckkkk!" I grunted as I murdered the pussy. Three days was just too fucking long for me to not be inside of her. I was beating her shit up like a nigga was fresh out of jail doing a bid. K'Yonnah was trying her best to keep up, but she couldn't. I smiled on the inside as I watched her pretty ass fuck faces. I had that pussy purring and her ass about to cry.

"Whose pussy is this?"

"It's yours, baby!"

"Who's the Boss!"

"You the Boss, baby! Yessss! You're the motherfucking Boss!" K'Yonnah screamed and started to squirt everywhere. Moments later, I was releasing all of my fucking seeds inside of her. I knew for a fact that was a baby right there. I could just feel my little niggas hitting their target.

******

I had been contemplating telling K'Yonnah about me being knee-deep in the drug game. I knew that I had to tell her because I didn't want her to find the shit out from somewhere else. Most niggas would rather keep their business dealings to themselves, but not me. I want K'Yonnah to know what the fuck is going on in case I get murdered or have to do a bid. I would go crazy knowing she was out in the world lost and not knowing what the hell to do. K'Yonnah was very book smart, but not street smart. I personally think that all women should be both book and street smart. That shit makes the perfect relationship.

"What are you doing here?" K'Yonnah asked as I walked inside of her office. The last time I was here was when I fucked the shit out of her. I still laugh at Shannie catching us in the act. K'Yonnah was so damn embarrassed.

"What? I'm still banned from coming to see you?" I laughed as I handed her a bouquet of roses.

"Ha-ha-ha! Very funny. Thank you, bae. These are so pretty." She grabbed my face and kissed me passionately on the lips.

"You want this dick on your lunch break?" I said as I grabbed my dick.

"No, Karion. You have me screaming too loud. You can definitely put it in my life later tonight."

"I got you, ma."

"Now what's going on? You only come to my office when you need to talk about something important. I'm all ears." She sat back in her chair and watched me intensely.

"I just wanted to tell you how much I love you and how grateful I am to have you in my life. Thank you for stepping up and taking care of Miracle. Not to mention how great you are with Lil Boss. I'm so proud of you, Yonnah. Look at you, bae. You've overcome all of the obstacles that have been placed in your way. Your organization is thriving and you're a successful business woman. I admire the fuck out of you. I sleep next to you every night and I feel like you need more."

"Karion, as long as I have you and the kids, I have everything that I need. This is the happiest I've been in a long time." K'Yonnah had gotten up from where she was sitting and sat on my lap.

"That's not what I mean. You deserve more from me than to just be a mother to my children. I need you to be my wife." I removed a blue Tiffany box from my jacket pocket and opened the box. I had purchased her a stunning three karat Tiffany Lucida engagement ring.

"Oh my God! It's so beautiful." She buried her face in my shoulder and began to cry so hard. That scared a nigga because I didn't know if she was happy or sad.

"Damn, ma! Is that a yes or a no?" I lifted her face and wiped her tears.

"Of course it's a yes, Karion. I'm crying because I'm so happy. When I was in prison, I dreamed of being with you and having a family. I never thought this would happen. I love you so much, Karion, and yes, I will marry you."

"She said yes!" I yelled and her office door opened and all of her staff, the residents, Kartier, Shannie, my OG, and the kids came inside clapping.

"I'm so happy for you!" Shannie said as she hugged K'Yonnah.

"That's what up, lil bro." Kartier and I dapped it up and exchanged a brotherly hug. I popped a bottle of Ace of Spades and drank right from the bottle. I leaned back against the wall and marveled at seeing the smile on K'Yonnah's face. I couldn't wait to see her beautiful face as she walked down the aisle. I was without a doubt ready to spend the rest of my life with the leading lady in my life.

Chapter 18- K'Yonnah

It had been two weeks since Karion proposed and I couldn't stop looking at my ring. From time to time, I would pinch myself to make sure this wasn't all a dream. It's like Boss is too good to be true. Even after all of these years of him being here for me, I still can't fathom it. I'm just so blessed and thankful to have him in my life. I don't know where I would be without him in my life. That man takes away every doubt and every fear that I have inside of me. There are times when I wake up in the middle of the night and watch him sleep. I stroke his face and kiss his lips over and over again. It's like he's my comfort zone. He makes everything better without really knowing that he does. I look into his eyes and I know the love he has for me is genuine. I know that he's telling the truth when he tells me that he will always take good care of my heart. It's crazy how you can love someone so much that you give your heart to them. My heart is not my own as long as I have Boss. He not only has the key to my heart, but to my soul. Every day he gives me a reason to wake up and make him happy. I want to cater to him in each and every way. Boss is the type of man who needs all of his needs fulfilled and I intend on being all that he needs until death do us apart.

*****

It was Lil Boss' seventh birthday and I had been running around like crazy trying to get everything in order. He loved wrestling so it was WWE themed. It was hell trying to find all of the decorations that he wanted, but I was able to pull it off. I was so excited because this was his first birthday party that I was going to be able to throw him. I was definitely going all out for my baby. It was his day and he could have whatever he likes. There was absolutely no expense or budget.

Lil Boss wanted BBQ for his guests so I needed to grab rib tips, chicken, burgers, bratwurst, and steaks to throw on the grill. As soon as I got in line, I remembered that I forgot to pick his cake up from the bakery. After I grabbed it and placed it in the cart, I ran dead smack into another person's cart. My heart sped up fast as I looked into the cold black eyes of Stone's mother. She looked even eviler than she did the last time I saw her in court when I received my sentence.

"It must be nice to celebrate your son's birthday," she said as she peered over into my cart to look at the birthday cake.

"It must be nice to celebrate your daughter's birthday," I told the old bitch. She must have forgotten that she had a hand in killing my daughter. As I stood before her, I became angrier and angrier. I was so mad I could cry. In my head, I was reliving that night I banged on her door until my knuckles bled to get my daughter. She refused to open the door. Instead, she called Stone on me. He came and beat my ass before sending me home. The next morning, my baby was dead. So, this bitch better get the fuck away from me before I murder her ass. The hatred I had in my heart for this bitch made me want to murder her ass and send her to see her evil ass son.

"I see you still got that smart ass mouth. Maybe I should hit you in it like my son used to."

"I wish you would try. I would murder your ass like I did your son. Get the fuck out of my way bitch!" Before I knew it, I had knocked her on her ass. She's lucky I was on parole or else I would have most likely killed her ass with my bare hands. After paying for my items, I headed home to get the food prepared for the party.

As I drove home, I found myself on the old block that I lived on with Stone. The house was still there. After all, I owned it outright. It was once my parents' home. Had I known what I know now, I would have run far away from that motherfucker. I was seventeen and didn't have a clue. All my life my mother and father basically spoiled me and I didn't have to lift a finger to do anything, but that shit didn't help me after they passed. I had no idea how to function in the world without them because they never taught me how to live without them. That's why it was so easy for Stone to come in and fuck my head up. I never thought there was life past the one he had shown me. That was until I crossed paths with Boss. Even though we only had a couple of months to be around each other before I went to prison, I had learned so much from him. Boss had the strength and tenacity I needed in order to survive. From the moment I met Stone, he was always feared by people, but not Boss. Boss had that nigga shook and I could see it in his eyes. It was the same look I possessed when he would beat my ass. It was funny how the tables turned so quickly. Boss gave me the strength I needed to pull that trigger. That and the fact that he had a hand in killing my daughter. As tears roll down my face, I quickly wiped them because there was no need for tears anymore. I had been sitting and contemplating what I was going to do with the house. It was paid in full and my banker kept up the mortgage while I was away with the money I inherited from my father. Stone's slick ass thought he had depleted it all, but he didn't. As I looked at the house, I knew that it held so many bad memories of what Stone did to me. At the same time, the house had seventeen years of beautiful and loving memories. The life I shared with my parents, I'll always hold near and dear to my heart. Not even everything that I had been through after their death could tarnish those memories. I no longer felt the need to hold onto the house. I would much rather donate it to a family in need of a home to call their own. Boss has given me and my son a life beyond my wildest dreams, so there's no need for me to hold onto the past because my present and future is very bright with him. I drove away from that property and headed over to the bank to sign the deed over to Nikkita. She was in need of something to call her own and I looked at her and saw me inside of her. We were very different, but alike in so many ways. It's like when you see someone going through something that you've been through, it makes an imprint on your heart. I love my son more than anything in this world and I can tell Nikkita feels the same about Paris. It's only right I make life a little better for her.

Lil Boss' party turned out to be a success. He ate so much BBQ, cake, and candy that he made himself sick. I was happy things went off without a hitch. With the emotions I had gone through early in the day, I knew that Boss could sense something was wrong with me, but I didn't want him worrying so I had to put on a brave face to keep him from asking me questions.

I had been so wrapped up with taking care of the kids and things at the office that I had forgotten to do something for myself. I was in desperate need of a massage, full set, and pedicure. I invited Shannie for a spa day and some much-needed girl time.

"Oh my God! That shit feels so good!" I said as Ming massaged my legs. Her hands felt like heaven as she beat them and placed hot towels on them. Shannie was over in the chair getting her nails filled in.

"Your name K'Yonnah, right?" the chick sitting in the chair next to me said.

"Yeah, it is. Do you know me? Cause I don't think we've ever met before."

"We don't know each other personally, I just heard a lot about you from your son's father, Boss. Tell him Natalie said what's up," she said with a grin on her face. I instantly became pissed off. I pulled my phone out of my purse and called his ass. I put the phone on speakerphone so this bitch could hear him. I wanted to know what type of relationship they had because this bitch had me all the way fucked up.

"Yooooo! What's up, bae?" he answered.

"Funny you ask me that. Especially since your little friend Natalie wanted me to tell you what's up."

"Really?" You called him." She laughed.

"Hell yeah, I called him. This my nigga so when another bitch is telling me some shit about how she knows so much about me, not to mention the fact that you saying he was telling you about me, I need to get to the bottom of the shit. Now he on the phone, so tell him what's up yourself." This bitch was really laughing like some shit was funny. I swear I was about to reach over and fuck her ass up.

"All of that ain't necessary. Boss and I are just friends from high school. I was actually your son's Pre-K teacher and all he ever did was talk about you. I'm actually mad because he left out the part about you being crazy as hell. We're cool, though." She laughed and paid the girl who was doing her pedicure. I felt so bad about my behavior.

"Hello," I said when I got back on the phone.

"I'll see you at home, K'Yonnah." He hung up before I could even respond and I knew that he was mad at me. I didn't think about how it would make him feel.

"Who is that chick you were over here talking to?" Shannie asked.

"Apparently, she was Lil Boss' preschool teacher and I thought it was more to it because she was speaking like Boss had been sitting up talking about me or some shit. Like the way she came off was like they fucked or something, so I called Boss and inquired about the bitch."

"No, you didn't. What did he say?"

"That he would see me when I get home."

"Bitch you in trouble." She laughed.

"I know right. Stop laughing, bitch; this is a matter of life or death." I managed to laugh and joke about it, but I was seriously scared as hell. I had no idea how mad Boss was at me. The tone of his voice alone had a bitch spooked.

I stalled with Shannie as long as I could before I finally had to head home. Boss' car was parked in the driveway when I pulled in. I took a deep breath and got out to go inside of the house. When I walked in, Boss was sitting on the sofa, smoking a blunt. I didn't even have the courage to say anything to him. I could feel the anger radiating off of him from where I was standing. I felt so bad, but my pride wouldn't let me apologize off top. I walked up the stairs to check on Miracle. I knew that Lil Boss was staying over a friend's house for a sleepover.

When I walked inside of Miracle's room, she was lying in her crib wide awake. She was eating her little hands up; a true sign that she was hungry. She already had premade bottles inside of the refrigerator I had inside of her room. It was hell going downstairs in the middle of the night to make bottles. I grabbed a bottle and placed it in the bottle warmer to knock some of the chill off of it.

"Hi, mama. What have you been doing with Daddy today?" I said as I rubbed my nose against her cheek. She was such a good baby and I just adored her beautiful self. Each and every day she was getting healthier and stronger.

After feeding, burping, and changing her, she was fast asleep and would most likely sleep until morning. That was another thing about Miracle; she would sleep well through the night. I would have to wake her up so that she could get her late night feeding. After tucking Miracle in and making sure her princess night light was on, I went to go and find Boss. I needed to woman the fuck up and apologize. I should have never called him or came at the chick all hardcore. I wasn't really a jealous woman. It was more so me knowing that my nigga is some of these other bitches' dream come true. I look at how bitches basically mind fuck him when we're out together. He doesn't pay those bitches any attention, but at the same time, I don't like the shit. Sometimes I wish that he would check those bitches, but I know niggas don't do shit like that. When I walked down the stairs, I was surprised to see that Boss had left. I looked out of the living room window and his car was gone. I knew he was mad, but he knows not to leave the house without at least saying something to me. A part of me wanted to cry, but instead, I grabbed a bottle of wine and poured me a tall glass. I was in desperate need of a drink at the moment. After drinking a couple more glasses, I was a little too tipsy and needed to lay down. I wanted to try my best to wait up for Boss, but the Sangria had made me tipsy. I took a quick shower and laid it down. Hopefully, he comes home soon so that I could apologize to him.

Chapter 19- Boss

I was so fucking mad at K'Yonnah for the stunt that she had pulled. For her to even carry on like that with some random female had me livid. I think what made matters worse was the fact that she didn't even apologize or justify her actions when she walked in the crib. Her calling me to prove a point to another bitch or question me about a bitch makes me feel like she doesn't trust a nigga. If she doesn't trust me, then there is no need for us to get married. Shit like this can't be happening. K'Yonnah knows that she is my baby and there is no other bitch out here that can have me the way she does. All I want to do is make life great for her. I rode around for a couple of hours checking on my blocks and trying to clear my head before heading home. I was angry and the last thing I wanted to do was raise my voice or argue with my baby. I was regretting just walking out like that. I never leave home without kissing my girls or my son. That shit makes me have a great day because I know they'll be there when I come home. I just want K'Yonnah to understand that she never has to prove herself to a bitch when it comes down to me, us, or where the fuck we stand. What's understood never has to be explained.

When I made it home, K'Yonnah and Miracle were both knocked out. The bottle of wine that was out on the coffee table explained why K'Yonnah was out of it so early. She's not even a drinker like that so I knew that she was lit. I kissed her on the lips and laid next to her. A nigga was tired as fuck. CoCo had been flooding us with merch and we were working around the clock getting that shit off. I had been working off of four hours of sleep a day and the shit was starting to take a nigga down. I'm not complaining, though. I'll sleep when I'm dead. Right now I gotta make this bread and make sure my family straight.

The next morning, I woke up to the sound of Miracle crying. I jumped up quick because it was one of those cries that sounded like she was hurt. When I rushed in her room, my heart stopped because K'Yonnah was on the floor unconscious. Miracle was lying beside her so that meant she passed out while holding her.

"K'Yonnah! K'Yonnah! Baby, wake up!" I was shaking her and I smacked her a couple of times to try and wake her up. She began to stir around a little bit and I breathed a sigh of relief. I immediately got on the phone and called for an ambulance; I couldn't take any chances with her or my daughter's life. If she passed out, it was obvious that something was wrong with her. Miracle had stopped crying since I had picked her up, but I still wanted to get her checked out to be on the safe side.

"What happened?"

"Bae, you passed out holding Miracle. Come on so you can go to the hospital and get checked out. The ambulance is on its way."

"Oh my God! Is she okay? I'm sorry, Karion. I don't know what happened. One minute I was getting ready to feed her, and the next I felt lightheaded. That's the last thing I remember up until now."

"That's why we're going to the hospital right now to see what the hell is wrong. That's not good at all." I lifted K'Yonnah up from the floor and carried her downstairs. I placed her on the couch and went back up to get Miracle. I hit my mother up and told her to meet us at the hospital. The ambulance was taking too damn long to come, so I ended up driving them myself.

I was on pins and needles waiting for the doctor to come in and tell me some news. Miracle had already been looked at and she was fine. My mother had taken her home with her. Now I was just waiting to see what was up with K'Yonnah. When they got her vitals, her blood pressure was high. That was most likely what caused her to pass out.

"Can we just go home, Karion? They're taking too long. We both know it was most likely my blood pressure. I've been working long hours and taking care of the house without a break. I'll just have to start allowing your mom to come over and help like she's been trying to."

"Hell no! We not leaving up out of here until they tell us exactly what the hell made you pass out. I need to know that you're okay. I'm glad you were home when it happened instead of outside somewhere or driving. Chill out, Yonnah. We have to find out what's going on, Yonnah. I can't lose you, ma." I bent down and kissed her on the lips.

"You're not going to lose me. I promise I'm not going anywhere." She wrapped her arms around my neck and hugged me. Seconds later, the doctor came back in and I was glad. I needed her to tell me something.

"Sorry to have you guys waiting for so long, but I think we found out why your blood pressure is so high. Congratulations, Mom and Dad, you're pregnant."

"No! That's not possible. I took four different pregnancy tests a couple of weeks ago and they were all negative." I looked at K'Yonnah like she was crazy because she had never told me that she thought that she was pregnant.

"Sometimes that happens. The only for sure way to find out pregnancy is through the blood. Lay back so we can do an ultrasound to see how far along you are." I shook my head at K'Yonnah but I remained calm because I didn't want to upset her. I held her hand as the doctor performed the ultrasound. I kissed the back of her hand, listening to the heartbeat. It was strong. In my heart, I could feel that it was a boy.

"You're about twelve weeks, Ms. Kyles. It's too early to tell the sex, but the baby looks healthy. My concern is your health and if you're taking care of yourself at home. High blood pressure is serious during pregnancy. Your levels are pretty high and my goal is to get them to come down because I don't want you to develop preeclampsia. I want you to take it easy. Make sure you take your prenatal vitamins and your iron pills every morning. It's imperative that you take care of yourself and the baby Ms. Kyles. If you don't, I'll be forced to put you on bed rest until you give birth. Here are some pamphlets and info about how to care for yourself during your pregnancy. Here is my card and your prescriptions. If you would like, I would be more than happy to be your OB-GYN. Get you some rest and call my office if you need me. Do you guys have any questions for me?"

"No. I think you pretty much covered it all. I will call you if we need to. I can assure you that I will make sure she takes it easy."

"That's great. She definitely needs a big support system. Congratulations again." We shook hands and she left out.

"Don't be mad at me. I didn't tell you because it was negative. At the time, there was so much going on with Meesh passing and Miracle being in the hospital. I just felt bad about being pregnant in the first place." She quickly wiped her face but kept her face covered with her hands. I removed them so that I could look her in the face so that she could see the seriousness in my eyes.

"I'm not mad. I just wished that you wouldn't have been afraid to tell me. Regardless of whatever the situation was, you were still carrying my baby. I feel like had you told me that you thought you were pregnant, you probably wouldn't have passed out this morning. Make this the last time you keep something from me like that. Now get dressed so I can get you home. I'm thinking I need to hire a housekeeper and a damn nanny. I don't want you lifting a finger. We also need to find someone to help Shannie out more at the center. I don't want you doing anything and this is not up for discussion."

"I'll let you be the man and put your foot down. However, I absolutely do not want a housekeeper or a nanny in my fucking house around the kids or you. I will kill a bitch if she even thinks about trying to tempt you or turn the kids against me." I couldn't so shit but laugh. This is why I don't like her watching Lifetime or the ID Channel. She's always thinking about crazy shit.

"We'll have my momma come and stay there with us to help out." I helped her get dressed and we headed home. The closer we got, the more I started to think about us getting married sooner than later. I was no longer comfortable with just being her baby father.

"I know that you want a big wedding, but I want to marry you ASAP. You're pregnant with my baby and I want to be your husband when you give birth, not your fucking baby daddy. We did that shit already and I want things to be different. Let's hop on a plane to Vegas and get married this weekend."

"Are you serious?"

"Dead ass. Just me and you. We can have a big reception and make it the baby shower too."

"Okay. Let's do it. Shannie is going to be so mad at me, babe."

"It's good. We'll get her a nice gift. We have to tell Ma though because she will have the kids. You just meet me at the altar in your white dress. I'll handle everything else." I grabbed her by the face and kissed her passionately. I'm so glad she said yes. I have to pull this shit off for her. She's not going to suspect a thing.

Once I dropped her off, I headed over to holla at Ma Dukes and my brother. I instantly became heated seeing my pops, Big Karter, sitting in the kitchen, holding my daughter. This nigga forever popping up out of the blue. From my understanding, he's supposed to be some type of agent for the government so he lives under the radar. I used to believe that shit when I was a youngster, but that shit getting old to a nigga now. His ass is more of a deadbeat to me. What government agent don't foot the bill for his seeds? I hate that my mother has always made excuses for his shit. When I was younger, it didn't bother me, but now that I'm grown and a father as well, the shit is not acceptable. Although he and my mother aren't together anymore, I swear when he comes around, she's like putty in his hands. I should call her boyfriend on her ass right now. Walking around the kitchen in her damn booty shorts and her shirt tied up in the front. Fuck calling her Ms. Miller; her ass was looking like Ms. Parker.

"Don't you think you should have on some clothes?"

"My name is Lena, not K'Yonnah. You can't tell me what the fuck to do. For the record, I do have on clothes."

"What's up, son? You're just the man I need to see. I just got off the phone with Kartier and he's on the way over. We need to have a sit-down." He placed a kiss on Miracle's forehead and placed her back inside of the bouncer.

"What exactly do we have to have a sit down about?" I didn't have time for his shit. I was trying to get to Vegas and get married.

"Wait until Kartier gets here. Trust me, he needs to hear this shit."

"He needs to hurry up. I got shit to do." I leaned over in the bassinette and adjusted the big headband Miracle had on her head. I hated those things. They looked so uncomfortable on her small head, but my momma and K'Yonnah didn't care. They were always buying her shit to make her look like a little diva. All I wanted was for her to look like a damn baby. She's only five months wearing skirts and shit. They making her grow up too fast and I don't like that shit.

"What did the hospital say about K'Yonnah? I'm worried about her health. She can't be passing out with those kids in the house with her. That shit ain't safe, Karion."

"That's actually why I came over, Ma. K'Yonnah is pregnant and her blood pressure is too high. She's been overworking herself. I just want to take her away and make it be all about her. We're going to Vegas this weekend and getting married. I don't want her to give birth to our baby and she's not my wife. She deserves better than that."

"Awww, son. I'm so proud of you. I'm glad you want to do the right thing by her. That girl has been through a lot. I would be lying if I said that I wasn't upset about you guys not having a ceremony." I walked over and wrapped my arms around her. I loved my momma. My brother and I spoil her rotten so she tends to get whatever she wants. After all, she has always taken care of us and given us whatever we wanted.

"Of course you're going. I need your help getting everybody out there. Talk to Shannie so she can help with the dresses and all of that. She knows what K'Yonnah likes. I have K'Yonnah thinking it's just us going out there. She has no family, so I know it will mean a lot to her if the family was there.

Here's my card, charge whatever. There's no budget for my baby. I want that shit real lavish, Ma."

"Yayyy! I get to plan this wedding. Let me go call Shannie right now." She kissed me on the jaw and rushed out of the room.

"I'm glad you're back on your shit, son. Your mother told me how you had shut down after the passing of your daughter's mother. I'm glad you found love in your son's mother." He patted me on the shoulder and bit the tip of his cigar.

"Me too."

"What's so important that I had to get out of bed? I was about to Netflix and chill with my wife."

"This is a matter of your freedom. Let's go in the basement and talk. Lena's nosey and I don't want her worrying." That piqued my interest because what the fuck did he have to tell us that would make my momma worry. All of a sudden, I became weak at the stomach. It was like I could feel he was about to lay some heavy shit on us. Shit was just looking up for a nigga. Bad news is the last thing I need right now.

"Damn, Big Karter! What's good?" Kartier asked.

"It's been brought to my attention that y'all fucking with CoCo LaRue."

"And?" I said.

"You two motherfuckers got a problem. She's under investigation with the Feds. Anyone who does business with her is also under investigation. I was working a case out in Florida and one of my colleagues was speaking on the recent surveillance he did and she had new niggas from the Chi. With further digging, I found out that y'all were the niggas in question. Now they don't have any evidence of you guys purchasing shit from her or distributing it on the streets, which is a good thing, but the bad thing is that she knows that she's on their radar. CoCo should be moving in silence, which she is now that she has you to do it. We've been investigating her for the last year, but every time we come for her, she seems to disappear. Not to mention all of the niggas that she fronted dope to have been arrested.

My guess is she's a snitch or there's a snitch in her camp. We need to figure out who's the leak before you niggas be in jail for the rest of your lives."

"We can't just cut ties like that," Kartier spoke up.

"I didn't say cut ties."

"Then what exactly are you saying? We all know that bitch is ruthless. Ain't no way she's just going to let us out of our business deal like that. The shit you speaking on can get all of us murked. While we're at it, I'm going to need you to come clean about whatever the fuck it is you really do. We grown as fuck now. You can stop with that secret agent shit." This nigga had me questioning everything he was saying. Shit sounded so suspect to me. I gave Kartier that look and I knew he was thinking the same thing.

"Let's just say that I put drug dealers away and take their shit afterward. That's all y'all need to know. I keep it the way it is because the less you know about me, the less danger you or your families will be in. After all of these years of being under the radar, I've still gone undetected. I can see it in your eyes that you don't trust me. Just know that it's because of me you've never seen a day in prison and you never will if you allow me to help you. When all of this is over, we'll be very rich. Go to Vegas and get married, son. When you guys get back, we can put our plan into motion. I have a job out in Baltimore and I can't miss that. Congratulations, son. I love you both. I'll see you when I get back." Just like that, he was out the door again. I just stood there leaning on the desk, shaking my head. It was always some shit with this nigga.

"Do you believe his ass?"

"I hate to admit it, but I do. At the same time, there has to be more to this shit than what he's telling us. The good thing about it is that we've already done our shipment and paid her ass for the month. When he comes back, we'll see what's to this shit. In the meantime, I need you and the family to come to Vegas with me for my wedding."

"I thought you were going to wait until the summer."

"We were, but I found out K'Yonnah was pregnant this morning. I don't want her bringing my seed in the world and I'm not her husband. Time wasn't on our side when she got pregnant with my son. I just want to make her happy, bro."

"That's what up. I'm so fucking happy for you. Of course we're all in."

"It's a surprise. She doesn't know that y'all are coming. I got her thinking that it's just her and me. We're going to stay at Caesar's Palace. You know they have different towers. I'm sure we can all stay there just keep in touch so that we don't run into one another.

"Okay, cool. When do leave?"

"First thing in the morning." We dapped it up and parted ways. I tried my best to think about getting married to the love of my life, but my father's revelation was heavy on my mind. I had a feeling he was going to come in and shake some shit up, but I was going to be ready.

Chapter 20- Mrs. Karion "Boss" Miller

I was in complete awe of all the sights and bright lights of Vegas. I know that I looked so crazy to Boss, but I had never been out of town besides the time he took me to New York for a couple of hours. This was like the best experience ever for me. The airplane ride alone was so exciting. I was a little sick at first, but it quickly subsided. During the flight, Boss kept my feet in his lap and massaged them. It felt so good for him to cater to me. At the same time, his ass was getting on my nerves acting like I was an invalid. Boss didn't want me doing anything. He was getting on my nerves already and I still had six more months to go.

The last thing I thought was that I could be pregnant. I had no symptoms or anything. After taking the tests and them coming back negative, I never thought about it again. I was glad he wasn't mad at me for not telling him that I had taken the tests. The last thing I wanted was for him to think that I was keeping secrets from him. From the moment he put his foot down and said that he didn't want me working, I had been thinking about how I was going to be able to run my organization from home. Boss was dead ass serious about me not lifting a finger. I knew without a doubt Shannie could handle things, I just didn't want to put all of the work off on her. She still has a husband and kids to take care of. I knew that Nikkita could definitely do it because she had been helping out around the center. I loved how she wanted to be a part of the team, but Kartier was still unaware of her being back in the Chi. Besides that, I was also worried about how I was going to be able to take care of a toddler and a damn newborn. My thoughts were running rampant and I knew that I had to stop all the negative thoughts or the shit was going to drive me crazy. Worrying wouldn't do anything but make my blood pressure high. I needed to just focus on having a healthy pregnancy. I didn't want any issues or complications. Boss was already out of his mind with worry and I didn't want to put that burden on him again. I can tell that he's scared I might not make it or something. I could tell by the way he was hovering over me. After all he had been through, he deserved not to worry, so I have every intention of making sure this pregnancy goes off without a hitch.

*****

I was so nervous I was shaking as I put on my wedding dress. Reality was setting in that no one was here with me. I think what bothered me the most was the fact that my mother or father weren't here. All girls want their parents to be at their wedding. I bowed my head and said a prayer for them. I also asked them to watch over me as I take on this next step in my life. Things were starting to look up for me. After so much pain and hurt, I was finally finding my happy place. I thanked God that Karion put a smile

back on my face and love in my heart. I placed my hand over my stomach and asked God to cover my unborn child and to bring him or her into the world healthy.

A knock on the suite door jarred me from my prayer. I quickly said "Amen" and wiped my face.

"It's me, bae. Can I come in?"

"No, Karion. It's bad luck to see the bride before the wedding." I leaned my back against the door, trying to make sure he didn't come in.

"I just wanted to let you know that I love you more than anything in this world and I'm thankful to have you in my life. From the bottom of my heart, I don't know where I would be without you. I want you to promise me that you will never question my love for you. I want you to know that no matter what we go through, you have my whole heart, K'Yonnah. I used to think that I knew what love was, but I never truly knew until you came into my life. Just when I thought we were going to be happy and be together, you went away and I couldn't cope. I had to move on, but I never stopped loving you. When you came home, I fell in love all over again. I'm so fucking happy we're getting the happily ever after we deserve. I just want to make you the happiest woman for the rest of your life. I love you so much, K'Yonnah." Just hearing Boss confess his love for me so passionately had me crying like a damn baby.

"I love you too, Karion. I want to make you happy for the rest of your life as well. I never in a million years thought that we would be getting married and on the road to spending the rest of our lives together. We're getting ready to have another baby and it feels so good to make our family whole. I promise to be the best wife and mother that I can be. You have to promise me that you will never keep anything from me and if you feel the need to cheat, please talk to me. Communication is everything in a marriage. Karion, I want us to have the type of relationship that no one else around us understands.

No matter what happens when we're mad at each other, we have to make a pact that no matter what we will never go to bed mad or without apologizing." I opened the door and slid my hand out so that we could hold each other. I simply didn't want him seeing me before the wedding.

"You got all of that and more. Now meet me at the altar in your white dress. A nigga ready to give you his last name." He kissed the back of my hand and quickly walked away. I quickly wiped my face and touched up my makeup, making sure not to get any on my beautiful dress. I was still in shock that Boss knew the exact dress I wanted. He had even gotten me a nice ass pair of all white Giuseppe slippers because he knew I couldn't really walk in heels, thanks to Stone breaking both of my ankles. I looked over at the box that was wrapped up on the bed. It was a gift from Boss. The note it came with had strict instructions not to open it up until I was dressed. I sat on the bed and opened the box slowly. Boss was going to have my ass looking fucked up walking down the aisle with all of these surprises. Inside of the box were four different items with small notes attached. The first item was something old and it was an antique silver pendant necklace from his grandmother that had passed. The second item was a brand new pair of diamond teardrop earrings. The third item was something borrowed and it was his mother's diamond tennis bracelet that she never takes off. The fourth and final item was something blue. It was a piece of one of my son's receiving blankets. His name and birth date had been stitched into the piece of fabric. It was the little things like this that made me never regret falling in love with Karion. He makes me feel so special. Like what woman wouldn't love a man that gets everything prepared for her special day. I received a text from the wedding planner who found us the venue and a Justice of the Peace. In Vegas, you can get all types of shit at short notice. I checked myself in the mirror to make sure my makeup was flawless and there were no loose strands of hair. I closed my eyes and prayed once more in silence. God had us covered in the blood. There's no way He can let us down now. I have faith that everything will be okay. I'm more than ready to become Mrs. Karion "Boss" Miller. As I headed towards the chapel, I had to take a closer look.

"What are you doing here, Kartier?"

"Now you know I couldn't let my favorite sis walk down the aisle without me being there to give her away." He held his arm out and I latched on to him and we headed inside of the chapel.

As I walked inside of the small chapel, I covered my mouth in shock. Boss had once again surprised a bitch to tears. I tried my best to hold the tears in, but I couldn't. The sound of the music playing made me cry more. Boss had gone all out. What was supposed to be a simple ass ceremony turned into a lavish ass ceremony.

Chapter 21- Boss

For you I'd give a lifetime of stability

Anything you want of me

Nothing is impossible for you

There are no words or ways to show my love

Or the thoughts I'm thinking of

The sound of "For You" by Kenny Latimore played as I watched K'Yonnah walk down the aisle. The look on her face was priceless as she saw my mother, Shannie, Kartier, our kids, and some of our close family and friends. Seeing her crying had me crying. Yes, your boy was shedding tears looking at his future walking down the aisle in the most beautiful Swarovski crystal-draped wedding gown. The gifts that I had given her complemented her skin quite well. Her hair was pinned to the side with a beautiful crème flower in it like the late great Billie Holiday. K'Yonnah had that beautiful pregnancy glow about her. My baby's melanin was popping. I couldn't wait for her to make it down the aisle. I walked my ass down to meet her. I grabbed her face and gave her ass the juiciest kiss filled with love and passion. Our guests were clapping and whistling, cheering us on.

"Let's get this show on the road. This young man is ready to marry his bride!" the pastor said, causing us to break our kiss and walk up to the altar. We grabbed each other's hands and faced one another. Seconds later, the pastor began to speak.

Dearly Beloved, we are gathered together here in the sight of God and in the face of this company to join together this man and this woman in holy matrimony, which is commended to be honorable among all men, and therefore is not by any to be entered into unadvisedly or lightly but reverently, discreetly, advisedly and solemnly. Into this holy estate these two persons present now come to be joined. If any person can show just cause why they may not be joined together, let them speak now or forever hold their peace.

Marriage is the union of husband and wife in heart, body, and mind. It is intended for their mutual joy – and for the help and comfort given on another in prosperity and adversity. But more importantly, it is a means through which a stable and loving environment may be attained.

Through marriage, Karion and K'Yonnah make a commitment together to face their disappointments, embrace their dreams, realize their hopes and accept each other's failures. Karion and K'Yonnah will promise one another to aspire to these ideals throughout their lives together through mutual understanding openness and sensitivity to each other.

We are here today before God because marriage is one of His most sacred wishes to witness the joining in marriage of Karion and K'Yonnah. This occasion marks the celebration of love and commitment with which this man and this woman begin their life together. And now through me, He joins you together in one of the holiest bonds.

Who gives this woman to this man?

"I do." Kartier kissed Yonnah on the cheek and we dapped one another before he headed over to his place next to Shannie.

"The bride and groom have decided to exchange their own vows. The bride will say hers first."

"I stand before you, our family, and most importantly, God, promising forever. There are so many things in life that I regret, but meeting you isn't one. You came into my life when I needed you most, but it wasn't our time then. Life stepped in the way, but it changed our future for the better. God has given us a second chance at love. For the rest of my life, I promise you that every day I will love you more than I did the day before. You've given me everything unselfishly. Never wanting anything from me but my love. And on this day, I give you not only my love, but my heart, my body, and my soul. You're so much more than the father of my children and my future husband. Karion, you are my life and with this ring, I vow to be with you the rest of my life." K'Yonnah slipped the ring on my finger and softly kissed my lips. It was now my turn to tell my baby exactly how I felt.

"If someone had told me the beautiful pregnant chick that I rescued would one day be my wife, I would have told them they were lying. From the moment I laid eyes on you, I knew you were special. There was something in the universe that God had planned for us. No matter what, we just kept running into each other. Then one day we both took a leap of faith. That leap of faith showed me just how much you meant to me. In an instant, you were snatched away before I could ever fully love you the way that you deserved. Now that we have a second chance, I'm never going to let you go. You're stuck with a nigga, Yonnah. I promise to always be the best husband I can be and give you whatever your heart desires. You're my world and all I need in this life is you and our kids. They say the first seven years of marriage are the hardest, but I say nothing formed against us shall prosper. Our love can conquer anything. You're the best thing that has ever happened to me and with this ring, I promise to make you the happiest woman in the world for the rest of our lives." I placed the ring on her finger and wiped the tears that had fallen from her eyes.

"By the power invested in me, I now pronounce you man and wife. You may now kiss your wife." K'Yonnah and I kissed and solidified our union. After all of the trials and tribulations, we were officially Mr. and Mrs. Karion Miller. It had been a long time coming, but it was well worth the wait.

Chapter 22- Nikkita

I had been back in Chicago for two months and things were going great. Shannie, K'Yonnah, and I had become so close. I was now an advocate at the center and I enjoyed helping out the other women because I could relate to what they were going through. It made me feel so good to be able to reach out to the women before they did something they would regret.

I thought killing Cord would make me feel better, but that shit was starting to take a toll on me. I was constantly looking over my shoulder like he was following me. I was having nightmares about his ass climbing out that grave and coming for my ass. The only thing that was keeping me sane was the fact that I had been able to spend time with my daughter.

Thanks to Shannie. Kartier was still unaware that I was in Chicago. I was so glad that Paris knew that her daddy couldn't know that I was around. I never thought that Shannie and I could become as cool as we are. I hate to say it because it is so awkward, but she's my friend. Most women hate their husband's baby momma, but Shannie has never made me feel that way. I knew she was a different type of woman when I knocked on her door and revealed that Kartier and I had a child together. I wore gym shoes and put Vaseline on my face because I knew she was going to want to brawl. Shannie handled herself better than any woman, including me. I'm forever indebted to her and K'Yonnah for helping me out of my situation with Cord. If it wasn't for them, my ass would be in prison.

I was so grateful for K'Yonnah offering me her home, but I politely turned it down. Not because I didn't want it, but because she had done more than enough for me. I didn't feel comfortable taking her parents' home from her. She tried her best to tell me that she didn't want it because there were so many bad memories in it. Not to mention that's where she killed her ex. I could look into her eyes and tell the house had sentimental value to her. I just couldn't take it from her.

My mother and I had recently reconciled and I was so happy. My mother didn't know that I had in fact killed Cord. She thought that I had just walked away of my own free will. That was all she needed to know. My mother was nosey as hell and she would probably tell all of her damn friends what I did. She wanted me and Paris to come and live in her guest house. I was cool with that, but I would be the only one moving in. Paris was going to continue staying with her father and Shannie. During our many visits, she told me how she loves her daddy and Shannie. They're over there spoiling her rotten. When she talks about Kartier, her eyes light up. I wouldn't dare try and take her away from him. After all, he's missed out on so many years. It's only right I allow him and her to bond and build their relationship.

*****

"What are you doing here?" I asked as I walked into my mother's house. Cord's mother was sitting on the sofa next to my mother. I was so damn scared I could have shitted right there in the foyer looking at this bitch.

"I'm here because I can't find my son. I've been calling his phone over and over, getting no answer. That's not like him. Where is my granddaughter?"

"You mean my granddaughter. She ain't got a lick of you or your son's evil ass blood running through her veins. Now I'm gone say this one more time; we don't know where your son at and we don't care." My eyes bulged out of my head listening to my mother read Cord's mother her rights.

"I know that your daughter knows where my son is. I also know that he is here in Chicago. I tracked his phone and it's here in Chicago. As far as Paris not having me or my son's blood running through her veins, she's more ours than yours. Where were you or her deadbeat daddy when she didn't have a pot to piss in or a window to throw it out of? Listen to me and listen to me good. I know my son has met with foul play and you know something about it. I'll be back and next time, it'll be with the police."

"Get your fat ass out of my house threatening my daughter before I fuck you up. I hope his ass is dead. He wasn't shit but a woman beater. I hope he's in hell and the Devil is putting hot shit up his ass." My mother yanked her ass up and threw her out of the door.

"Thanks, Ma. That lady is crazy and out of her fucking mind if she thinks I have a clue where Cord is. I'm just happy he doesn't know where me or my baby is." My mother narrowed her eyes at me as she flamed up a cigarette.

"Get your ass over here and sit down, Kita."

"What's wrong, Ma?"

"Cut the bullshit. Your ass is lying. Now you see, that fat bitch doesn't know you, but I birthed you. When your ass is lying, your eyes change colors.

Now tell me what the fuck is going on." I put my head down in my hands and braced myself before I revealed the truth.

"I'm sorry, Ma. It was an accident, but he deserved it. He was beating my ass and he revealed that he had been touching Paris. I didn't know what to do, but I knew I couldn't let him get away with hurting her. When he finished beating me, I put some shit in his food that made him drowsy. Eventually, he went to sleep and I beat his ass with a bat until I killed him. I panicked and I drove his body from Texas. I knew that Kartier's wife, Shannie, worked at a domestic violence shelter. I went straight there and I told her I needed her help. She called her friend, K'Yonnah, who owns the domestic violence shelter. It just so happens she did time in prison for killing her abusive ex. We buried his body out in the Forest Preserve, Ma. It's off the beaten path; I can assure you no one will ever find his ass. I feel so stupid, Ma. He was hurting my baby." I fell over on the couch and cried my heart out. Every time I thought about that nigga, I envisioned him touching my baby.

"Shhhh! Don't cry, baby. It's not your fault. You did what you had to do for your baby, but you need to tell Kartier about this. Cord's mother is going to be a problem. I can feel it."

"I was thinking the same thing. I'm going to call Shannie so we can talk about telling him. I think we should do it together."

"I agree." I kissed my mother and I called Shannie on the phone. I knew that we could no longer keep it from Kartier. I just hoped he wouldn't be mad at Shannie.

Chapter 23- Kartier

Shit had been good for Shannie and me, but I couldn't help but have the feeling that she was keeping something from me. It's not even like me to not trust my wife. It's just that she keeps saying how she's been hanging out with a new friend, but never mentions the person's name. I know that she's been hanging out with someone because K'Yonnah is on strict bed rest and my brother is not letting her out of his sight. She's been working overtime at the center and a nigga misses the fuck out of her. For a minute, the thought of her fucking another nigga crossed my mind, but I quickly shook that shit off. Shannie wouldn't do any shit like that. Plus, her ass ain't crazy; I will kill her and that nigga.

"I can't believe your ass got me out here stalking your wife with you," Boss said as he flamed up a Kush blunt.

"We're not stalking. I just want to see what the fuck she up to. K'Yonnah has always been her only friend that she would actually go out and kick it with. I mean she had other friends, but she didn't fuck with them like she does with K'Yonnah. Now she has this new friend she hanging around with. I've never heard her say the person's name and that shit is suspect as hell to me. Now she told me she was going to meet her friend at White Palace for breakfast. I just want to see who she's with, that's all. Trust me, I'm going to keep my distance. The last thing I want to look like is a stalker. Then again, I don't give a fuck what I look like. As long as she ain't with no nigga, it won't be a problem.

"I hear you, bro. Shannie loves you, though. I don't think she's out with a nigga, so get that shit out of your head. Let's see what's good so I can get home and check on K'Yonnah. I think her ass sneaks and eat shit she's not supposed to when I'm away. I swear she's going to make me snap. The doctor gave her a list of food she can and cannot eat. She knows the baby's life and hers are in danger." Boss had been on edge ever since K'Yonnah passed out. I knew it was his fear of losing her like he did Meesh. I don't blame him because I would be the same way about Shannie if her life were at stake. I was getting ready to respond, but as we pulled up to the restaurant, I noticed Shannie walking her ass down the streets with Nikkita.

"Is that who I think it is?"

"Yeah. What the fuck that bitch doing in Chicago? As a matter of fact, what the fuck is my wife and my baby momma doing hanging out together."

"Just be happy their ass not at each other's throats. There has to be some logical explanation as to why they are meeting up in secret."

"Man, bro, what if they fucking?" Boss fell out laughing and hitting the dashboard. His ass was laughing like some shit was funny. I was dead ass serious, though.

"Nigga, get the fuck out of here! Shannie is not fucking Nikkita. Just go home and wait until she gets there. Come straight out and ask her what the fuck she's doing with Nikkita. Let's go before she spots your car." I quickly drove away because I didn't want her to notice my car. As I drove to drop Boss off to his car, I couldn't help but wonder what the fuck they were up to. I swear they better not be plotting on a nigga.

*****

"Come here, baby," I said to Paris when I walked in the house. She was sitting on the couch watching Disney Channel. Every time I look at my daughter, I beat myself up for missing out on so much of her life. If I could change the hands of time, I would and be the father that she needed.

"Hey, daddy."

"Hey, sweetie. Cut that TV off for a minute. I want to ask you something." Since she had been with us, I had been trying my best to get her to tell me about her life with Nikkita and that fuck nigga. I had hired a private investigator to go down to Texas and follow his ass. I wanted as much information on his ass as I could get. I also wanted him to keep eyes on Nikkita as well. He had been coming up short and now I know why. Her ass has probably been here for the longest.

"I'm going to miss my show, daddy."

"Stop that pouting. You can turn it back on after we finish talking." I lifted her up and sat her on my lap. She had her arms folded and her lips poked out. She's spoiled already. Thanks to my wife, she had Paris looking like a diva and acting like one as well.

"I'm going to ask you something and I want you to tell me the truth. You're not going to get in trouble from Mama Shannie or me. Have you seen your momma since the last time she left that nigga?" She put her head down and played with her fingers, something she did whenever the nigga's name was mentioned in her presence.

"Is he going to come back and get me?"

"Now you know your daddy will never let that shit happen. Are you scared of him?"

"Yeah. I don't want him to hurt me or mommy anymore." I became instantly heated just hearing the fear in her voice.

"You told me that he never hurt you. I know that you've been scared, but the only way Daddy can protect you and Mommy is if you tell me what he did to you. I promise that I will protect you from him. He will never hurt you again."

"He told me that he would kill me and Momma if I ever told anybody."

"Told anybody what?"

"He would make me touch him on his private. I don't want to say no more, daddy." She cried on my shoulder and held on for dear life. I held my baby and I cried too. I was so fucking angry that I wanted to kill any motherfucking thing in my path.

"Go upstairs to your room and finish watching your show. Everything is just fine and like I told you before, he will never hurt you again and that's a promise." She hugged and kissed me on the jaw and ran upstairs. I jumped up and rushed into my office. I needed to punch some shit or break something. I didn't want to scare my kids or alert my mother. I put my head down on my desk and shed more tears. I was so fucking angry I was hurt. I failed my daughter. Had I been the father I was supposed to be this shit would have never happened. Hell, I can't even be mad at Nikkita. That nigga was whooping her ass. Fuck letting that private detective find that nigga. I was going to have to take a trip down to Texas my motherfucking self.

The sound of the alarm beeping made me jump up and rush out of my office. I knew that it was Shannie and she was just the person I wanted to see. Heading down the stairs, I observed both Nikkita and Shannie sitting on the couch.

"Hey, bae."

"Cut the bullshit. What the fuck is going on? Let me guess, this is the friend you've been hanging out with." I grabbed a blunt from the candy dish I kept on the coffee table. I flamed it up and sat back on the table across from them.

"Please don't be mad at Shannie. I begged her not to tell you. I was just too scared of how you would react."

"I'm going to be mad at Shannie regardless. I'm her husband and she should have never hid the fact that you were here. Especially since my motherfucking daughter just told me that fuck nigga was sexually abusing her." I lost my cool and flipped over the coffee table, causing the glass to shatter all over the floor.

"Calm down, Kartier. Let us explain," Shannie cried.

"Don't tell me to calm down. Do y'all have any idea how this shit looks? Where the fuck that nigga at, Nikkita? I swear to God on every motherfucking thing I love I will beat your ass worse than that nigga ever did if you lie." I was now standing up over her and Shannie was trying to hold me back. Nikkita was shaking and crying, but I didn't give a fuck. She needed to tell me where that fuck nigga was at.

"I'm sorry, Kartier. I didn't know that he was sexually abusing her. I found out recently. He confessed while he was beating my ass. He made me fix him something to eat and I put some shit in it that would knock him out. When I knew that he was out of it, I beat his ass to death with a bat."

"Why the fuck didn't you call me? You can't be out here catching bodies and shit. You need to be out here for Paris. How long ago was this shit? I just know them people looking for you. So, you killed the nigga and fled here, huh?" I rubbed my temples in frustration as I thought about how bad this shit could turn out.

"I panicked and I drove from Texas to here with his body in the trunk. I didn't know where else to go. Shannie was my last resort." I looked over at

Shannie and I knew this story was about to go from bad to worse. She was sweating like a slave and biting her nails.

"If you drove up here with his dead body, then where the fuck did you put it?" I was starting to get frustrated with her ass.

"We buried him in the Forest Preserve," Shannie spoke. My eyes got wide as saucers because I was trying to make sure that I had heard her say "we".

"I had no other choice but to help her." I sat back and stroked my beard, looking at my wife and my baby mother. I didn't know whether I should be scared or proud. My baby momma had just murked a nigga and my wife helped her bury his body. Niggas love unity amongst the mother of his children and wife. At the same time, they hid some shit from me that I could have handled. *I really need to watch these bitches.*

"I need to go holler at Boss about this shit; we have got to get that nigga moved. As long as there is a body, there's evidence. I'm not going to snap, Nikkita, because you did what you had to do, but Paris is my seed. You should have called me the minute that nigga revealed what the fuck he had done. As for you, Shannie, you're my wife and you know better than to keep any motherfucking thing from me. I'll handle your ass later. Since y'all all friendly and shit, let's get this threesome popping."

"Don't fucking play with me Kartier Miller!" Shannie jumped up off the couch and slapped me upside my head.

"Nigga, please! You're my baby daddy and all, but you ain't even my type these days."

"Shit! It was worth a try. Let's ride out. I need y'all to show me where the fuck you buried this nigga at. I advise you to put on your digging clothes."

"For what?" Shannie asked.

"Y'all buried his ass, so you need to dig him up. I'll be there to assist you, though." I was dead ass serious. I needed to teach their asses a lesson. They wouldn't have to go through the shit again had they come and told me the truth from the jump.

Chapter 24- K'Yonnah

Life had been going so well for Boss and I. Being married to him had been so fulfilling. Lord knows I love him, but he is so damn overprotective. I can't pass gas without him questioning me about it. I hate for him to leave and go out to handle business, but now I welcome that shit. I never thought there would be a day I would be happy Boss wasn't at home, but he is driving a bitch up the wall. He won't let me go the bathroom in peace. I can't eat shit, and I'm so mad because he won't let me work. On the other hand, I loved how attentive he was to my needs. The foot and booty rubs feel like heaven.

This baby was giving me the blues. If I wasn't sick, I was sleepy. All I wanted to do was sleep. Although I was supposed to be on bed rest, I still had to do my motherly and wifely duties. I knew that Boss had to get up and make things happen for us. I find it quite comical that he thinks that I don't know he sells drugs. I'm not slow by a long shot. I just sit back and make him think I don't know what's going on. It's better for both of us. He doesn't like to put any worry on me or stress me out. For some odd reason, he likes to shield me from anything detrimental to me. He tries to protect me in every way that Stone never did. As for me, I feel like the less I know the better it is for me. Each and every time he walks out the door, I ask God to bring him back home to me in one piece. That's all I can do.

Since Lil Boss was at school, I decided to take a much-needed nap. It was important that I slept while Miracle slept. Lately, she had been staying up longer than usual and I needed the rest.

A couple of hours later, I woke up and headed to her room and immediately began to panic. She was gone from her bed.

"Oh my God!" I screamed as I looked all over her room. I ran towards the stairs to run down them but felt a hard shove in my back. I tried to hold on to the banister for balance, but I was kicked in my side. I grabbed my stomach as I fell down each and every stair. When I hit the bottom stair, I hit my head hard as hell on the floor and blacked out.

*****

The pain in my head was excruciating. I tried to focus, but my vision was blurry. It took me a minute to focus but when I did, I noticed that I was back in my old house that I shared with Stone. I immediately began to panic. When I tried to move around, I realized I was tied to a damn chair.

"Helpppppp me! Somebody help me!" I screamed and thrashed around in the chair, trying to get free.

"You can scream, but nobody can hear you!"

"What the fuck? Bitch, you better untie me." Stone's crazy ass mother had kidnapped me.

"Now is that any way to talk to your mother-in-law. You always were a disrespectful little bitch!" She punched me and kicked the chair over, causing me to fall.

"Please stop! Why are you doing this? Where is my stepdaughter? Please, she has nothing to do with this." All I could do was think about where Miracle was and my unborn baby. Stone's mother was standing over me with a shiny butcher knife.

"Shut the fuck up! You know exactly why I'm doing this. Did you think I was going to let you get away with killing my son? You knew he was my heart and you took him from me. Not to mention the fact that you have another man raising his son. Who in the hell is Miracle?" Now this bitch was two types of crazy if she thought my son was by Stone's deranged ass. My heart dropped hearing her ask who Miracle was. I just knew she had her here somewhere too. Something was off about all of this, but I had to stay on track and see where this bitch's head was.

"My son is not by Stone. His father is Boss, but you already know that. As far as me killing your son, he deserved that shit and you know it. You saw him beat me on several occasions. If memory serves me right, you called him to beat my ass the night I came to your house to get my daughter. What woman would stand around and allow her son to beat the shit out of his woman? Not to mention kill his daughter for insurance. You're doing all of this for what? That man killed my daughter and you're doing this to me because I took his life. Bitch, you are truly crazy. I swear you better do whatever the fuck you have to do because I will not beg you for my life. I'll die with my dignity before I ever beg a bitch like you for my life. Get the shit over with. I would love to go see my daughter and my parents."

"My son didn't deserve to die. He was supposed to lay hands on your disrespectful ass. I told him he should have killed your ass back when he first started fucking with you. You were weak just like your fucking mother." She charged at me with that big ass butcher knife and…

POW! POW! POW!

"No, bitch! You're weak just like your fucking son!"

"Ahhhhh!" I started screaming at the top of my lungs and scooting all around in that damn chair. I was still tied up so I couldn't get away. Stone's mother was lying next to me on the floor. Her cold black eyes open and the top of her fucking head gone. One would think that's what had me screaming, but it wasn't. I had pissed on myself because I was looking at a ghost.

"Get up, baby. It's okay. Let me get you out of here."

"You are not real! This is a dream!" I yelled. I closed my eyes tight because when I opened them, I wanted my mother, Karyn, to disappear. I opened my eyes and she was still there. I started to cry and vomit. I was hurt and sick to my stomach.

"Come on. I can't explain right now. You're bleeding, K'Yonnah. We have to get you to a hospital." I looked down and blood was dripping down my legs.

"Noooo!" I cried as my mother untied me from the chair. Besides knowing that I was losing my baby, I was trying to understand why my mother was here. I wanted an explanation, but right now, all I could think about was my husband and our kids. So much was happening at once and I didn't know what to do.

"Just calm down. Let's go. I'll explain everything later." She helped me out of the house and into her car. I sat in the passenger seat, crying my heart out. I just didn't understand what was going on. This morning I woke up the happiest woman in the world—life was perfect—and in a blink of an eye, things changed. In my heart, I knew that I was most likely having a miscarriage. Boss and I really wanted this baby. I didn't even know what I was going to say to Boss. I still had no idea where Miracle was. I looked over at this stranger because that's exactly who she was. I became angry at her presence. I had been through so much in her and my father's absence. She owed me an explanation that couldn't wait.

"Is Daddy alive?"

"Yes, he is." She wiped the tears from her eyes and all I could think was, *why the fuck is she crying?* I should be the one crying.

"I can't believe you guys have been alive all of this time. Do you have any idea what I've been through? You guys left me when I needed you the most. Stone beat my ass every day. He killed my daughter. I sat in prison for killing him. All of this was going on and y'all were somewhere living life without me. How could you guys do this to me?"

"I'm so sorry, K'Yonnah. It was never our intention to do this. When Stone cut our brake lines, he really did think that the crash killed us, but it didn't. We were pulled out of the car before it exploded. We were both fucked up. When I came to after about two weeks of being out of it, Red had already made it look like we were dead. That was for our safety and yours. There was so much going on with your father and his gambling debt. Stone was nothing compared to the LaRue Drug Cartel. Your father owed those crazy ass Mexicans a boatload of money for fucking up their drugs. I didn't know about the drug shit until after the accident. All these years we've been in hiding trying to get our life in order. There hasn't been a day we haven't thought about you or what was going on in your life. I hate myself every day for allowing your father's shit to take me away from you. As a parent, we were never supposed to just leave you like that. At the time, we were presumed dead so it was best that we kept things that way. Your father owed so many people. I knew if we ever came back, they would not only kill us, but you as well. I would die a million deaths every day to keep you alive, K'Yonnah.

We've been living in California and it's been hard as hell trying to be a good wife to your father.

He's out there doing the same bullshit he was doing here—gambling his life away and fucking over people. I've tried my hardest, but I can't do this shit anymore. He's going to fuck around and get himself killed for real this time. I can't sit around like I did all those years ago and act as if the shit is okay. He doesn't even know that I'm here. I hopped on a plane and came to get my baby and reveal the truth. I only came by the house to see if it was still there. That's when I heard you screaming. God put me there for a reason. From the bottom of my heart, K'Yonnah, I'm so sorry for all of the heartache and pain you had to endure in our absence. For the rest of my life, I'll do whatever I need to do to make it up to you. Right now I just want you to focus on getting to the hospital and getting checked out."

I put my head down in my hands and cried silently. I was going through so many stages of sorrow at the moment. I didn't know what else to do but cry. My mother, who was once my best friend, was now sitting next to me and I had no clue who she was. She was a complete stranger at the moment.

I could feel in my heart I was losing my baby, so I was trying to come to terms with the inevitable. My mind was racing as I tried to figure out where Miracle was. I would never forgive myself if something had happened to her on my watch. All I needed at the moment was Boss. By now, I knew that he was worried about me. I had no idea how long I had been out of it.

"I need to call my husband." I wiped the tears from my eyes as I spoke.

"I don't have a phone. I got rid of it so that your father couldn't call me. As soon as we make it to the hospital, we can call him. Everything is going to be okay, baby." She leaned over and rubbed my back as we headed to the hospital.

Chapter 25- Boss

My plate had been absolutely full trying to keep an eye on K'Yonnah and keep my business dealings going on with CoCo LaRue. Just like I expected, my father had disappeared again. He didn't even show up for the meeting that he had scheduled for us. I was pissed because all that I could think about was being snatched up by the Feds. Just like his ass to drop some heavy shit like that on a nigga and disappear. At this point, me and my brother were in limbo because the money was coming in by the boatload, but our freedom was possibly in question. I'm a husband and a father so my freedom is way more important. I have more money than I know what to do with. My businesses are doing well, my family is straight, so I have no qualms about walking away from this drug shit. I know whatever I'm with, Kartier is with, so we're good.

My intentions were to tell him that I was backing out of this with CoCo LaRue, but I got sidetracked by him telling me about Nikkita killing her nigga. It fucked me up in the head when he told me that Shannie had indeed helped Nikkita. That made me wonder if K'Yonnah knew about this or if she had helped them. I wouldn't put it past her if she did help out. She and Shannie are thick as thieves. Not to mention, she goes hard for all of the women who stay at the shelter. It empowers her to help women who have been in the same predicament as her. The way she advocates makes me so fucking proud of her. Knowing K'Yonnah, her ass was probably the mastermind. I've learned that she is far stronger and smarter than she lets on.

After I helped Kartier get rid of the nigga's body for good, I needed to head home and shower. What was left of the nigga was not a pretty sight or smell. All day my mother had been calling me, but I couldn't answer. When I finally did answer, she was telling me that she had been trying to get in touch with K'Yonnah, but she wasn't able to. Earlier that morning, she had come over while K'Yonnah was sleeping and took Miracle home with her. K'Yonnah had been overwhelmed lately with the pregnancy and the kids so she wanted to give her a break to have some alone time. She sent her a text telling her that she had picked up the baby, but she had yet to respond. That wasn't like her at all, so I started calling and sending her texts with no answer. I became alarmed because it's not like her not to answer the phone for me. I knew in my heart something was wrong. I headed straight home but received a call from a nurse telling me that K'Yonnah was at the hospital. I hauled ass trying to get there. All the while, my mind was racing with fear. I prayed that she and the baby were okay. About ten minutes later, I arrived at the Northwestern Hospital.

"Excuse me, my wife, K'Yonnah Miller, was brought in. She's pregnant and I need to find out where she is." I spoke nervously to the front desk attendant.

"Oh yes, sir. She just went up to the maternity ward. Take those elevators straight ahead up to the sixth floor. Let the front desk know that you're the spouse." She handed me a visiting pass and put it on. I rushed and caught the elevator just before it closed.

"Six, please."

"I know you. How's your wife? It was a miracle what happened to her. All of the labor and delivery staff are still coming to terms with her recovery." I was looking at this tall white man, worried about what the fuck he was talking about.

"No, my wife is fine, she's upstairs in the maternity ward."

"She must be visiting the baby." Him saying that made me look at him like he was crazy. What damn baby is he talking about?

"You don't remember me, do you?"

"No, sir, I don't."

"I'm one of the residents that helped deliver your wife's baby. We were working on her for twenty minutes trying to resuscitate her before we pronounced her dead. About forty-five minutes later, we were unhooking tubes and the nurse who was preparing her to go down to the morgue felt a faint pulse. We immediately went back in. Low and behold, she was alive."

"No. That's not possible. I saw her lying on that table and she was very much dead. I don't know what type of fucking games you're playing, but this shit ain't funny. My wife died and our daughter is home with me." I had stepped in his face because I was about to beat his ass. He grabbed both of my forearms in an effort to keep me from swinging on his ass.

"Calm down. Let's go into this conference room so I can explain things further to you." At first, I was hesitant because I wanted to get to K'Yonnah, but this nigga was talking about Meesh being alive. I needed to see what he was talking about. This shit had me on edge and worried. If what he was saying was true, then K'Yonnah and I weren't legally married. I was not prepared to tell her some shit like this. I'm just praying this is some type of mix up.

"What happened with your wife is called Lazarus syndrome. It's basically the spontaneous return of circulation after failed attempts at resuscitation. It's a rare occurrence, but there are a number of cases throughout the United States of people who were pronounced dead and were found to still be alive. I assure you your wife is very much alive. After she finally came to, we asked her if there was anyone that we should call and she called her mother. The next morning, I came on call because she left the hospital with her mother and an unknown male. We've been trying our best to find her. The child's grandmother was coming to see the baby. We weren't at liberty to discuss the patients' whereabouts because she wasn't listed as next of kin. Neither were you. I'm looking at you and I can tell that you had no idea about this. I'm sorry, sir." I sat trying to process this shit. Why would Meesh not want me to know that she was alive? She basically left our daughter.

"Thanks, I have to go." I quickly jumped up and walked out of his office. I made way to the other side to find where K'Yonnah was. Ironically, I bumped right into her and an unknown woman.

"Hey, babe."

"Are you okay?" I grabbed her and squeezed her tight.

"Yes and no. The baby is fine. I thought I was having a miscarriage, but they said that it's just my period. The placenta is still intact. After everything I've been through this morning, I'm surprised. Babe, I don't know where Miracle is. I'm sorry. I went to sleep and when I woke up, she was gone." K'Yonnah became hysterical and started to cry. I quickly grabbed her in for a hug.

"Miracle is fine. My mother came over to the house to get her while you were sleeping. You were sleeping so good she didn't want to disturb you.

What happened to you this morning? Why didn't you call me?"

"Stone's crazy ass mother kidnapped me. If it wasn't for my mother, she would have killed me."

"Your who?" I looked up at the woman standing off to the side, looking damn near identical to her. To my knowledge, her mother and father were dead.

"Hi. I'm Karen. Nice to meet you, Boss."

"Nice to meet you too." We shook hands and she walked over and whispered in K'Yonnah's ear before walking away.

"It's a long story. Let's just go home. I'll explain it later." She latched on to me and we walked out of the hospital. I didn't know what the fuck was going on, but apparently people are rising from the fucking dead around us. I have an eerie feeling that shit is about to get worse before it gets better. Just thinking about the revelation about Meesh's ass really being alive put me on edge. I didn't have it in me to say anything about the shit to K'Yonnah at the moment. I just want to get over to my mom's and get the kids and make sure they were cool.

"Let's go get the kids first and then we can head home. I need to make some calls to hire some security; this shit is fucked up. I feel like I've made you too accessible. There is no reason why that bitch should have been able to get into our home."

"I'm fine, Boss. I don't want a whole bunch of strangers walking all around the house. Plus, my mom killed her ass. I'm okay. I just want to get my kids." I grabbed her hand and kissed the back of it as I continued to drive to my mom's house. K'Yonnah had no clue of the evil that might fall upon us. About thirty minutes later, I pulled up to my mom's house.

"Why is the door wide open?" K'Yonnah asked.

"Stay here, Yonnah. Don't get out of this car!" I hauled ass getting out of the car and inside of the house. My heart dropped seeing my mother tied to a chair with her mouth duct taped and a note attached to her. I quickly pulled the tape from her mouth.

"Who did this shit, Ma?" She was crying and out of breath trying to talk.

"That bitch Meesh and her mother. They took the kids."

"What the fuck you mean they took the kids?"

"Yes! They were together. Meesh is the one who tied me up while her momma took the kids out of the house. How is this possible, Karion? That girl is dead."

"Stop crying, Ma. I'm going to handle this and get the kids back, I promise. As far as her being dead, we know now that she's not. I ripped the letter off of her and fell back on the couch to read it. Anger consumed me with each sentence that I read.

Thought you and that bitch were going to have a happily ever after, huh? Well, God had better plans. For me, that is anyway. Who would have known that I would be pronounced dead only to miraculously come back? Apparently, my death was a good thing because you married that bitch the moment you could. Consider that shit null and void because I'm very much alive. Last time I checked, bigamy was against the law. I'm not dead. Far from it, my nigga. Real bitches don't die, they go to Vegas and fuck up some commas. I'm back, I'm better and coming for everything that you denied me.

I gave you all of me and from the moment that bitch got out of prison, I became invisible to you. The bitch stood in the home that we shared lusting all over you as if I wasn't in the room. The sad part about it was that you openly lusted over her as well. I've seen women fall all over you, but she was different. That bitch felt a sense of entitlement to you and that made me hate her. It made me hate you even more because you let her know the shit was okay.

All of sudden, it's fuck Meesh. Fuck the fact that I had been more of a mother to her son than she was. There I was trying to fill the shoes of a woman I could never compare to in your eyes. You did a real good job at acting as if you ever loved me.

You hurt a bitch bad, but I intend to hurt you worse. See the thing I know you love most is your kids. Especially Lil Boss because she gave birth to him. I mean you motherfuckers made sure to remind me of that.

So here's how this is going to go. Miracle is my fucking daughter. I birthed her, not you or that bitch. What, you and her thought you were going to raise her as yall's daughter? I don't fucking think so. As far as Lil Boss goes, I might not have birthed him, but for five years, he called me Momma. That bitch been out for a year and wants to act as though she's always been there. I'm taking my kids and I promise you will never get them back. I want to see you cry, nigga. I want you and that bitch to suffer for the pain you caused me. Y'all started it, but I'm definitely about to finish it. They say hurt people, hurt people and I plan on doing just that to both of you.

"What's taking you so long, Karion? Oh my God! What happened?" K'Yonnah said and it made me hurry up and put the letter behind my back.

"I told you not to get out of the car."

"Stop the shit right now! Where the kids at?" She started going from room to room looking for the kids and crying loudly.

"Get her before she falls running like that," my mother cried out.

"Excuse me, I'm looking for K'Yonnah Kyles." Two officers appeared in the doorway.

"That's my wife. Why are you looking for her?"

"We have a warrant for her arrest." He handed me a piece of paper and it stated that she had violated parole.

"What's going on?" K'Yonnah came back into the living room. I looked over at the officer and he looked at the photo he had in his hand.

"Ms. Kyles, you're under arrest for violation of parole. You have to come with us."

"Nooooo! I didn't violate parole. There has to be some type of mistake. Do something, Boss."

"Stop crying, bae. I'll be down to the station to bail you out as soon as I can. Don't be so fuckin' rough with her. She's pregnant man." The officers were practically about to break her wrists putting the handcuffs on her.

"Lord have mercy, Jesus! Why is this happening, Karion?" my mother cried. I was going crazy trying to comfort her and my wife. All the while wondering how in the fuck I was going to get my kids from this psycho ass bitch. She could get ready because I was going to kill her and her fucking mother. That's on my life. K'Yonnah had done everything she needed to do in regards to her parole so I knew this was some shit Meesh was behind.

"Look, Ma. I need you to close the house up and put the alarm on. I just hit Kartier up and he'll be here shortly. Don't open the door for anybody. If you think somebody is trying to come in and it ain't him, shoot first and don't ask who it is." I handed her my gun and she took it.

"I wish I had this thing a little while ago. I would have blown those hoes' head off. Go see what's going on with K'Yonnah and get my grandbabies back. Be safe. Do you hear me, Karion?"

"Yes, Ma. I hear you." I kissed her on the jaw and rushed out of the door. I hopped in my car and hauled ass towards the precinct. About ten minutes into the drive, I was cut off by a huge black Yukon truck. I reached under my seat and grabbed my Mack. I didn't know who it was, but I was not taking any chances. The back door opened and CoCo LaRue stepped out, along with some of her goons. *What the fuck?* I had given this bitch my cut for the month, so she had no reason to even be here right now.

"What's good, CoCo?" I said as I stepped out of the car.

"Come and have a talk with me."

"Can this wait until later? I need to go check on my wife."

"Actually, it can't. Get in." She climbed back inside and her goons held the door open for me. I didn't know what the fuck was going on, but I knew it wouldn't end pretty for me if I didn't. I wasn't trying to die today. I needed to save my fucking wife and my kids. I climbed inside and sat next to her in the back seat. She was staring out of the window like she was in deep thought.

"Here, this is for you." She handed me a black hat box and I opened it.

"What the fuck?" I yelled as I threw the box on the floor. I immediately became sick. I had to open the window to vomit everything I had eaten. The feeling of her rubbing my back made me knock her fucking hand off of me. This bitch had just shown me my father's head.

"That's what happens when you go against the grain and bite the hand that feeds you. Your father was a rat for the government against my organization. After all these years of allowing him to make money with my family, he tries to turn my associates against me. I took it personally that he did that with you. After all, he knew the plan I had for us. All he had to do was get you to accept my offer. Instead, he had his own agenda. For that treachery, I wanted his head." I sat in awe looking at this bitch talk calmly like she hadn't just shown me my father's head.

"What plan is that?" This bitch was fine as fuck with Devil horns sticking out the top of her head. She reached over and placed her leg on my knee.

"From the moment I laid eyes on you, I knew I had to have you to myself. I can give you the keys to the whole city if you want it. The shit is yours for the taking. You can have the life you deserve. I'm just the bitch to give it to you. In my eyes, you're a king and you need a queen to take care of you. You'll be a well-kept nigga for the rest of your life. There's nothing you could want for, that Mama LaRue can't give. All I ask is that you let me feel that big black dick whenever I want it." She grabbed a handful of my dick and I quickly knocked her hand away.

"That shit sounds good, Coco, but I already have a queen in my life. My wife treats me like a king. I don't need to be a well-kept nigga. I stand on my own and make sure my woman is well kept. As far as me giving you this big black dick, I can't because it belongs to K'Yonnah. Thank you for the offer, but no thanks. Now if you'll excuse me, I need to go check on my wife." As I tried to get out, a huge screen came down and came on. I gritted my teeth together looking at my wife sitting inside of what looked like an interrogation room with the same officers that arrested her.

"All I have to do is say the word and it will be as if she never existed. I can tell you love your wife a lot. So you will give me what I want when I want it."

"So you just gone make me give you the dick?"

"Like I said before, I get whatever the fuck I want. I know that you love your wife. I also know that you want your kids back. It just so happens I know of their whereabouts as well and they can be hand delivered to you. I'll make sure to bring your baby momma as well. So, if you scratch my back, then I'll scratch yours. How much do you really love your family?"

"I love my family more than life itself, but my dick ain't for sale. I will not betray my wife for you or any other bitch. I'll get my wife and my kids back." This bitch had me fucked up if she thought I was about to fuck her.

"Suit yourself." Before I had a chance to respond, I felt a sharp pain in my neck. My body became limp. I couldn't move, but I could see what was going on. Coco had unzipped my pants and started giving me head. That was the only way she could get it because I wasn't doing that shit willingly. I looked up at the screen and my eyes locked with K'Yonnah's. I guess there was also a screen where she was showing her what was going on. I tried to speak, but I couldn't. I moaned out. Not in pleasure, but from frustration of not being able to explain to her what was going on. I was now wishing I would have just given her the damn dick. My baby wouldn't even have to go through this shit right now.

"Why, Boss? I thought you were coming to get me! You promised you wouldn't hurt me! Cut it off! I don't want to watch it anymore!" The sound of her crying and wailing was the last thing I heard before I completely blacked out.

TO BE CONTINUED!!!!

COMING SOON
FROM MZ. LADY P

Married to The Mob

: A Black Mafia Love
Affair

Written By:

Mz.Lady P

Chapter 1- British Brooks

I'm wishing on a star. To follow where you are. I'm wishing on a dream to follow what it means.

As I lay in my bed I listened to the soulful sounds of *Wishing On A Star by* Rose Royce as it blasted through our home stereo system. It was Saturday night and my mother and her friends were playing Tunk for money. For as long as I could remember Saturday nights were designated for my mother her and her little crew. They would gamble all night until the early morning hours. In my opinion my mother and her friends had yet to really grow up. They acted like teenagers with no children to me. My mother Italy is forty five but doesn't look a day over twenty five. She is absolutely beautiful and stacked in all of the right places. She has the prettiest shade of caramel skin I've ever seen.

All the young niggas loves them some Italy. She thinks it's so cute that they call her old ass "Mrs. Parker."

In my opinion it's creepy as fuck but I love Ma Dukes. I've never had a hungry or fucked up day with her as a parent. I've never wanted for anything and if I did she made sure to get it the best way she could. I've never met my father and that's fine by me. In the words of my mother "fuck that deadbeat motherfucker." I could never miss a nigga I didn't know shit about. I've never even had a father figure in my life. Over the years my mother has had plenty of boyfriends but she never let them live with us or try to be a father to me. Italy didn't play that shit. I guess the only thing bad that I could say about my mom was that I wasn't allowed to call her mom. From the time I learned how to talk she instilled in me that I was to call her Italy. After a couple of times of getting my ass whooped for calling her "momma" I got the hang of things. Most people would frown upon that but it is what it is. Besides that Italy has been the greatest mother I could ever ask for.

At nineteen I really didn't have a social life. I would much rather spend my time at home in bed curled up with a good Urban Fiction novel. All I did was work, go to school, come home and read. I worked as a LPN at Rush Hospital and I was enrolled in Malcolm X College for Nursing. My schedule was completely full so I really had no time to party or hangout. As a matter of fact I really didn't have friends. I guess you can say I was a loner. Growing up I was the girl no one really wanted to hang with. It wasn't that I was ugly or dirty looking. I was the fat girl with the pretty face whose mother kept her in all the latest. I've never had a boyfriend or went out on a date for that matter. For some reason boys just didn't see me for who I was on the inside. I long ago gave up the dream of ever living a happily ever after.

Over the years I've slimmed up tremendously. I've gone from wearing a size 24 to a 16. I'm still considered to be a BBW but I'm more confident than I was back when I was wearing a size 24. Despite gaining some confidence my self esteem is still low in regards to my appearance. When you're belittled for so long and called fat it takes a toll on you mentally but I'm getting better. I think the hardest part about being a big girl is when a nigga say, "you're pretty to be a big girl." That shit is so confusing to me. Like is that a comment because I'm not hardly impressed. If all niggas came at me like that I'll continue to be a virgin. I refuse to give any of these ignorant ass niggas in the hood a chance at something so precious. My self esteem wasn't ad high as it should be but don't get it fucked up. I don't take no shit from nobody. Getting teased over the years has me quick to snap out but I'm learning to control my anger

My mother and her friends were good and drunk. Not to mention loud as fuck. There was no way I was going to be able to get sleep. With they asses singing loud and talking about how they needed dick. I swear they had no chill. As I grabbed my Kindle to find something to read my bedroom door opened and my mother walked in with a beer in her hand.

"Why are you in here by yourself? Come out here and keep Chloe some company?" I rolled my eyes because I couldn't stand her ass. Not when we were kids and not now either. She was one of those bitches who wanted to be your friend in private but not in front of others. I didn't need this sometiming as bitch around me. Her aura was too fucking negative for me. It was crazy how my mom and her mom Kesha were best friends and we weren't friends at all. Well we were when were younger at her convenience. That was until I had to kick her ass for talking about me behind my back to her friends. I haven't really fucked with her like that since. High and bye would suffice. She was and still is a fake ass bitch in my book.

"I'm good. You know I don't like her ass." A knock at the door stopped my mother before she could respond.

"Come in." I said.

"What's up B? I'm getting ready to head to this party for a little while. Do you want to roll with me?" I felt my mother nudge me before I could say no. On one hand I didn't want to go while on the other hand I was bored out of my mind.

"Yeah. I'll roll with you. Let me get dressed."

"I'll be outside in the car." I just rolled my eyes at her ass as she smiled like she had won the lottery. This bitch was up to something I could feel it.

"I'm so glad you're going out British. You are nineteen and be around here acting like you are fifty. You're beautiful and might I add thick as fuck. I swear you done dropped all that weight and it settled in all the right places. Walking around here looking like my sister instead of my daughter.

Go out and have fun with Chloe. You work and you deserve a night out to just kick it. Go get fucked up and find you some dick."

"Really Italy?"

"Hell yeah! You need to get out and live a little." Italy kissed me on the jaw and left out of the room. I just shook my head at her. She was hell bent on me losing my virginity. I jumped up from bed and grabbed me a tight fitting all white summer dress from my closet. I removed my bonnet and let my thirty inch weave fall down my back. I had already taken my bath so I was clean. I plugged up my flat irons and sat down in front of my vanity to put on my makeup. After applying my make up I put a few spiral curls in my hair. After throwing my dress on and placing a pair of Michal Kors slides on my feet. I gave myself the once over before heading out. I said a silent prayer that I didn't have to kill Chloe's ass tonight.

****

"I thought you said we were going to a party." I asked as I looked around this damn gated community that looked deserted.

"We are going to party. It's just not the typical parties that we're used to. This is the Demonte Estate. " Chloe said as she applied a fresh coat of MAC lip gloss to her lips.

"Who in the hell is that?" I was confused as fuck at the moment

"Wait a minute. You don't know who the Demonte's are?"
She was starting to piss me off.

"No the fuck I don't Chloe. So enlighten me."

"The Demonte's are one of the most ruthless and richest Crime Families in the Chi. Put it this way they're considered to be the newest era of the Italian Mob."

"Bitch is you crazy. Why in the hell would you bring me to some shit like this? Take me home."

"Oh my God British! Calm the fuck down. We're cool. I wouldn't bring you nowhere if it wasn't safe. Plus, I miss us being friends. When we were younger we had so much fun together. I hate myself every day for what I did back then. We're older now and I just want to make amends for everything. I'm so sorry British. Can we start fresh?"

"I guess so but I'm telling you now if you're on any bullshit with me I'm going beat your ass."

"Yayyyy! Now come on. So you can meet my baby and his family." We quickly got out of the car and walked up the long drive way to a huge ass house.

"You deal with one of these damn gangsters?"

"Yes I do. For the last six months I've been dating the youngest brother Dom Demonte. I swear British. I'm so in love with him. He makes me feel so good. I swear I want to give him all the pretty little mixed breed ass babies he wants." We both bussed out laughing and I welcomed that. I forgot how crazy this fool was. Her eyes lit up as she talked about him. I was happy for her but a part of me was jealous as well. I longed to have someone to make me feel the way Dom makes Chloe feel. I quickly shook my thoughts away from my head as we walked further up the driveway. I would never have something like that.

"Good evening Ms. Chloe." A man said who was had on a black suit with an earpiece in.

"Hi Joe. This is my friend British."

"Hello beautiful. Welcome to the Demonte Estate." He opened the massive double doors and ushered us in. My mouth dropped to the floor looking at interior. It was all white everything with nothing but pretty chandeliers making the entire room light up. He showed us out to the backyard and I was astonished at the posh surroundings. It looked like a pool party for the rich and famous. There were ice sculptures, Cabana's draped in white and rhinestones,

Waiters and Waitresses serving everybody. The only thing that stood out to me was the fact the people were black. I could have sworn Chloe said these people were a part of the Mob.

"Why are all these blacks folks at this party?"

"Because these black folks are the Demonte Crime Family. Oh shit! I forgot to tell you they are half Italian and Black. Their father is Italian and their mother is black. Just chill and close your mouth. Act like you belong in this motherfucker! There goes my baby right there". She grabbed my hand and we walked closer towards a group of men. There had to truly be God because these men were fine as shit. They were all so handsome. All of them were rocking long beards and low cut fades. They were some beautiful ass men. They looked like black men but you could tell they were mixed with something by their light skin tone. I immediately begin to become nervous standing in front of them. I looked down at my feet and started to pull at my dress. Chloe jumped in her boyfriends arms and he picked her up off the ground spinning her around.

"Hey Babe. Sorry I'm late. I had to go pick my friend up. This is British. British this is my boyfriend Dom, and his brothers Corleone and Lucci.

"What's good Ma?" He said and I held my hand out to shake his but he pulled me in for a hug.

"Sup. I'm Lucci." He gave me dap and knocked back the drink he had in his hand. While the other brother Corleone gave me a head nod and walked away. I rolled my eyes at his rude ass and continued to just stand there.

"Don't pay my brother no mind. Make yourself at home. Let me steal my baby for a minute." He wrapped his arms around Chloe's waist and they walked inside the house. I just stood there looking crazy as ever. I wasn't really a drinker but at the moment I needed something to calm my nerves. I grabbed a glass off of a tray as a waitress walked passed. I looked around and noticed that one of the Cabana's was empty. I walked inside and sat on the plush white sofa. I looked around at all the people that were in attendance. They all looked rich as fuck. I felt out of place and I could tell they knew I didn't belong. Chloe needed to hurry the fuck up before I called UBER and took my ass home.

*****

Four glasses of Champagne and hour later I was still sitting alone. Chloe ass had yet to come back outside. I knew that she most likely fucking but she needed to bring her ass on. I didn't know a soul at this party. I was tipsy and regretting ever coming with her ass. I sat scrolling through my phone when I looked up and some black creepy ass nigga sat beside me on the sofa. He was so damn close he might as well been sitting in my lap.

"What's up beautiful? Do you want some company?"

"Not really." I sipped on another shot of Champaign but continued to ignore his ass.

"Well fuck you then. Fat ass bitch!"

"The bitch is the one who pushed your extra ugly ass out of her pussy!" I responded but without warning he drew back his fist and punched me in my face.

"Motherfucker!" I quickly reached in my purse and grabbed my Taser. His ass didn't know what hit his ass. He immediately fell to the floor and I tased his some more until he pissed on himself.

"What the fuck is wrong you?" I felt myself being yanked back. When I turned around it was Dom's brother Corleone.

"Nigga get your fucking hands off of me."

"Who the fuck you think you talking too?" He roared stepping in my face. His eyes looked like they had turned black. I quickly cowered because this nigga looked crazy as hell towering over me.

"Oh my God! What happened to you British?"

"This nigga punched me in my fucking face so I tased his ass." I felt something wet on my lip. I looked down and noticed that I had blood all over my dress.

"Get your bitch ass up!" Dom yanked the nigga off the ground and quickly started whooping his ass. Lucci and Corleone jumped in and did the same. I was starting to feel light headed so I needed to sit down.

"Hold your head back B. This shit is coming out in clumps. You might have to go to the hospital. I sat with my head back in disbelief. This is exactly why I stay my ass in the house. I don't have time for this bullshit here.

"Just take me home. My fucking head is banging." I said with an attitude. I really didn't mean to be snappy at Chloe because it wasn't her fault. I was just ready to get the fuck out of here. The ride home was quiet. I didn't want to talk. I just wanted to go home and forget this day ever happened.

Chapter 2- Corleone Demonte

If it wasn't one motherfucking thing it was another. I can't never have one night where I can just chill and enjoy the fruits of my labor. What was supposed to be a mixer for potential investors turned into a fucking bloodbath because we whooped this nigga Spook's ass for the shit he pulled with Chloe's fucking friend. Now we have to have a sit down with our father and fucking explain what the hell happened.

Despite our father stepping down he still finds away to run shit. He's groomed us to run the family but is never satisfied with the way we do things. So there is always some type of fucking argument or disagreement between him and I. With me being the oldest he puts a lot of pressure on me and pressure makes diamonds. So I shine in everything that I do. I think that's what fucks him up the most. I run shit better than he ever did.

My father Salvatore DeMonte was born into the Mafia. His father was Don Matteo Demonte. A strict full blooded Italian man who believed firmly in his Italian beliefs that he bought over with him from the old country. He raised my father with those same beliefs so that he would one day run the family just like his father before him. He was groomed to run the family but all of that changed when he met our mother Dina. He fell in love with her and became pregnant with me. Nothing would have been wrong with that had she been an Italian woman. She was black and from the projects and that was the ultimate shame in regards to Italian heritage. They didn't date outside of their bloodline. Because my father did so and refused to abandon my mother he was disowned but that didn't deter him. He started his own faction of the Demonte family and built a powerful empire. As much as I hate my father at times I also admire him for following his heart and staying with my mother. It's thirty years later and they're still together going strong with four kids to show for it.

******

"Where are you going Corleone? I thought you said you were going to spend the day with me and CJ."

"What the fuck I tell you about questioning me? In case your ass forgot I have an empire to run. How many times do I have to remind you Sasha?" I turned back around in the mirror and continued to fix my tie.

"I'm sorry Corleone. It's just that I hardly ever see you and you never come home at night anymore. I miss you so much. I just want to get back to our happy place." Sasha was sounding so pitiful and that shit disgusted me. If there was nothing I hated more about a woman it was a needy one. Sasha has the world at her feet. Access to my money, private jet, homes, cars, and whatever the fuck else she wants. Somehow her ass is never satisfied. After the birth of our son CJ the shit got worse and her ass has become a turn off. That accompanied with her excessive drinking. Sasha was the true definition of a bad bitch. She was beautiful, thick as fuck, and fucked like a porn star. Unfortunately, her ass has turned into a fucking drunk pussy. That shit is a complete turn off because the Chardonnay was starting to seep through her pores. I hated lying next to her because I could smell that shit. It was only a matter of time before I gave her ass her walking papers. The only thing that was keeping me with her was our son and pretty soon that wouldn't be enough. I can't even bring myself to fuck her because I'm so turned off. I would rather jack my dick to porn. I love pussy and pussy definitely loves me.

"I understand that you miss me but I have work to do. Don't wait up" I kissed her on the forehead and quickly walked out of the bedroom. I kissed my three year old son CJ on the forehead and prayed over him as he slept. As I descended the spiral staircase I observed Sasha opening a bottle of wine and pouring a huge glass. I just shook my head at this bitch drink the wine straight down. A lady is suppose to sip wine not drink it like it's a damn beer. Watching her guzzle the wine gave me the confirmation that I really need to cancel this bitch. I don't give a fuck about us being together for ten years. Shit just wasn't working for a nigga anymore.

*****

"Are you gone make love on the phone or join this fucking discussion?" I swear ever sense Dom hooked up with Chloe his ass been on that sprung shit. I like her for him though. She keeps his nutty ass out of trouble.

"Chloe got the little nigga sprung."

"Man fuck y'all bitch ass!" We all laughed because even as a grown up. Dom hated to be teased. Especially when it comes down to his precious Chloe.

"You young ladies done." My father said as he stroked his beard. His demeanor alone was letting me know that this meeting was not about to go well. This was one of the things that I didn't like about his ass. He always went the extra mile to be sarcastic and down right disrespectful.

"Sorry about that Pops." I looked over at Dom when he said that and narrowed my eyes at his ass for saying that shit.

"Now what the fuck happened here last night. Those were some very important people that were here last night. We've been working for months trying to get those people to sale their homes to us."

"It's simple Spook disrespected a female and hit her in her face like she was a fucking man. In return she tased his stupid ass and we beat that nigga ass. Now as far as the investors goes we've already set up a private brunch for us and them." Lucci explained.

"Who was this lady anyway?"

"She was my girl Chloe's friend."

"You have a girl. Why haven't you bought her to meet me and your mother."

"I wasn't ready for all that but I'll bring her by soon."

"Not soon this Sunday. Now back to Spook. He works for this family and he's your mother's nephew. It's up to you to explain to you aunt why her son is in the hospital with broken ribs and broke back. "

"I'm not about to explain my actions to no motherfucking body. That shit was justified. End of discussion. I got shit to do. I'll holla at ya'll later." I got up and walked out. I refused to sit and discuss this meaningless shit. Plus I had this brunch I was putting together for these investors. I give less than a fuck about Spook and that's real. He had been fucking up money and I simply couldn't have that shit on my watch. Blood or not his ass was collateral damage. You have to get rid of those types before they dismantle all of the hard shit we've worked so hard for.

******

"Yeah that's right you nasty bitch! Suck that dick just like that." I said as I looked down at this bitch that was giving me some good ass top. I pulled her hair up from her face so that I could see her pretty ass lips. They were glistening from the thin coat of MAC lip gloss she applied prior to eating this big motherfucker.

"Mmmmm!" She moaned as I begin to fuck her face roughly. Not long after I was cumming all down her throat. She happily sucked a nigga dry just the way I liked it.

"Good girl. You know how to do that dick just the way I like it. Now go finish putting the finish touches on this brunch I'm having later. Don't fuck this shit up Maya or I'll fire your ass!" I smacked her on the ass as she rushed out of my office to do her real job. Maya was my Administrative Assistant and my personal dick doer. Yes, this bitch was wicked with filing and swallowing my kids. I couldn't have hired a better fit. Doing my dick was all she could ever do. I would never slide my dick up in her ass. If she was swallowing her boss dick with no problem she had no qualms about passing out that pussy. I was good on her in that way plus I like my bitch's nasty and classy.

My phone chimed as cleaned my dick off. I looked at the screen and it was a video message from Sasha. I opened it and it was a video of her fucking the shit out of a dildo. That shit sounded like macaroni and cheese being stirred. Her shit was so creamy. Surprisingly, my dick rocked up but as soon as she talked it got soft.

"Come home and make love to me." She slurred. I quickly closed the message and through my phone against the room. It fucked me up that Sasha had become a fucking drunk. I chose her to be the mother of my child and this is how she behaves. I should have listened to my mother when she told her ass was unworthy. I was young, dumb, and thought I was in love. The saying that mother knows best hasn't rang more true. I hated to do it but I needed to part ways with Sasha. Our relationship was officially over. All I needed was for her to be good mother to our son and if she couldn't do that. I would without a doubt terminate her parental rights. My son was a Young King and would be raised as such. It's best I cancel that bitch. I'll get me a new one.

Chapter 3- Chloe Conners

Things between Dom and I was getting serious and after six months of dating he wanted me to move into his home with him. The only problem with that was my mother Kesha. She was dead set against me being with Dominic Demonte. I hated that she judged each and every nigga I came in contact with on a personal level. At twenty I've had my fair share of men but they were nothing like my baby Dom. He treated me better than any man I had ever been with. He makes me feel so sexy and beautiful. I never been with a man who compliments me continuously through out the day. Sometimes I didn't think I was good enough to live in his world. After all his a rich kingpin and I'm just a chick from the hood living from paycheck to paycheck. At first I didn't feel like this but my mother insists on reminding me of how superior Dom is to me. Nothing hurts my feelings more than her telling me that I'm just something to do until he finds a real bitch on his level. When she first said that to me I cried. What type of mother tells her daughter some shit like that? Mines that's who. With her judgmental ass.

Despite being hurt by her words I refuse to let it deter me from the happiness and love I've found with Dom. It's a honor to live in his world even it turns out to be short lived. For now I'll act as though it's forever with us.

"Where you on your way to?" My mother asked as she lit a Newport.

"I was invited to Sunday dinner with Dom's family." I looked in the floor length mirror and did a once over. I was nervous as ever meeting his parents for the first time. I wanted to look presentable so I wore a nice pants suit with a pair of heels. I placed a thin coat of makeup on. I didn't want to put the shit on all thick and be looking like a happy hooker.

"Don't go over there thinking just because those people invited you to dinner you're apart of their family. You're beneath them Chloe and you could never fit in with them damn Demonte's."

She took a pull off of her cigarette and put it out." I rolled my eyes at her ass as she walked out of my bedroom. She lived to put me down. I guess that's why it was so easy for me to be mean to British when we were younger. My mother made me out to be a mean girl and in return I ended up not having any friends. The older I've become I realized that British was always a good friend to me. I'm so happy that she has decided to give our friendship a chance. I know I don't deserve it but I plan on doing everything I can to prove I've changed. I'm so damn happy she ain't mad at me for the shit that happened at the party. It would have crushed me had our damn new friendship ended before it begin.

I'm so happy they whooped Spook's black ass. He's a bitch nigga for hitting British like that. His ass didn't know what hit him when she tased his black ass. Watching my baby whoop that nigga ass made me horny ass hell. One thing about my baby and his brother's they didn't take no shit. They were the cause of the damn murder rate. One would think that would make me steer clear from Dom but that only made me want that nigga more. At twenty five he was tall, sexy, and handsome as fuck. I love tugging on his long beard that he took great care of. Those beards were like the Demonte trademark. I think that's what made me attracted to his ass. It was something about that damn beard that made me want to ride his face like a surfboard and drench it with my juices. That nigga had turned my ass into a freak and I loved every minute of it.

******

"It's so nice to finally meet you Mrs. Demonte. Thank you for having me over for dinner." Mrs. Demonte and I were sitting out in her garden sipping wine and having general conversation. Dom was in his father's office discussing business.

"Likewise Chloe. I'm so happy my baby boy has finally found him a good girl to call his own. It's about time he has found him a good girl and not them tramps he was keeping company with. I would have killed him had he bought one of them to my home. Allowing us to meet you let's me know that he's serious. That and the fact that he wants you to move on the Demonte Compound." Her last statement piqued my interest. I knew that he wanted me to move in with him but not on his family's massive private property. Dom, Lucci, Corleone, and their parents all had their own homes out on the outskirts of the city away from people. Their sister Ava Marie is away at college but she also has a huge home on the estate as well.

"I thought that I would be moving into his apartment in the city." I said a I sipped my wine.

"Oh no! You're his woman now. Being in the city is a risk for you and him. I've never been the type of woman to sugar coat anything so I" keep one hundred with you as my sons would say. It takes a strong woman to be the woman of a

Demonte man. There is no room for the weak or the vulnerable. My boys need strong women to marry and bear their children. If you want to one day become his wife you must be the strength he needs. He doesn't need a ride or die bitch. He needs a woman that can't sit back observe, speak when spoken too, and be his security when shit gets hectic. Trust and believe me it will get hectic. Jail time is a possibility, Death is a great possibility, there will be other women. You just learn to play your role and play it well. Never let another woman bring bullshit to your door step. I'm sorry if I'm being so frank but had I learned all of these things in the beginning my marriage would be one of love and not convenience. Listen to your future mother in law you have to be prepared for whatever when you're Married to the Mob. " I sat quietly in deep thought taking in everything that she had said. She made it all sound so hard to be with him. Yes, I love Dom but I didn't want being with him to be a full time job. Although her words were weighting heavily on my mind and heart it still didn't deter me from being with Dom Demonte. It was either build a life with him or exist with my mother. I choose Dom.

"Dinner is ready Mrs. Demonte." The housekeeper said. She grabbed my hand and we walked inside together. I guess she could tell I was a bit nervous so she squeezed my hand tightly.

"Look at my two favorite girls bonding." Dom smiled as he stood to his feet and pulled my chair out. His father did the same for his mother. It was my first time getting a good look at their father and I could see where him and his brothers get their looks.

"She's a great girl Dom. I think she's the one." His mother said as she leaned over and kissed him on the cheek.

"Great choice son. She'll make beautiful sons for you." His father said in his raspy voice. I cracked a smile because I didn't want to give off the impression that I didn't want to give Dom babies. Everything is happening so fast. For the rest of the night we ate and conversed. By the end of the night it was decided that I would be moving onto the compound that weekend. I really had no say so because Dom was adamant about me moving in ASAP.

*****

"What's wrong Ma? You've been quiet since we left dinner. Did I do something?" Dom said as he reached over and grabbed my hand. We were in his car and he was headed to drop me off at home.

"I'm okay."

"Don't lie to me. What's wrong with you?"

"I don't know. You don't think we're moving too fast do you." Dom hit the brakes hard as hell in the middle of traffic.

"Hell no! We're not moving too fast. At least I don't feel like that. You came into my life at a time when I needed you most. There are so many bitches out here that I've allowed to entertain me or I just used for a quick nut. I've fucked with bad bitches on every fucking continent but none of them move me like you do Bae. Are you having second thoughts about moving in with me?"

"I want nothing more but to move in with you. I just want to be able to live up to your family's standards. No. Let me rephrase that. I want to be the woman you need me to be. In your line of work I know that you need me to be strong and I don't want to disappoint you. I don't want you to wake up one day and regret choosing me. I know we're not married or anything but just being the girlfriend of Demonte is important." I quickly wiped the tears that had fallen.

"I need to keep your ass away from my OG. She got you all worried and shit. Look at me Chloe. You are not my mother and I am not my father. You fuck with me because of who I am as a man not because of what my last name is. Just continue loving and fucking with a nigga the way you have been. Stop worrying. I know that you're everything I need and more. You'll be just fine." He reached over and we engaged in a passionate kiss.

The cars behind us were blowing so that we can move but we didn't give a fuck. My nigga was assuring me that everything would be okay so they ass would just have to wait.

Chapter 4-British

My face had finally healed from that motherfucker hitting me in my shit. By the grace of God he didn't break my nose. He did however black both of my eyes. I missed a full week of work behind that shit and I was more than ready to get back to the money. Since I had missed so many hours and I needed the money I decided to take on double shifts. The ER was short staffed so I was placed down there to give them a helping hand on the 11 to 7 shift. The whole damn city of Chicago must have been sick because the ER was packed to capacity. I braced myself and prepared myself for a long night. I grabbed a chart from the reception desk and called a patient. I did a double take looking at the name on the chart before calling it.

"Corleone Demonte Jr." I yelled loudly. I looked around and a beautiful woman holding a little boy's hand stood up. It didn't take a rocket scientist to see that he was indeed Corleone's son. It's amazing how he had strong features just like his rude ass daddy.

"Right here!" I stood waiting for her to make up to the where I was standing and I ushered them into a cubicle to get them checked in.

"What's going on with this little one here?" I placed a thermometer in his mouth and a blood pressure cuff on his arm. I sat back in front of the computer and jotted down as she explained his ailments.

"I don't know. One minute he was fine and the next he was acting like he couldn't stand and he was slurring with his words. On the way over he vomited a couple of times in the car. He doesn't have fever so I don't know what it is." After entering his temp and blood pressure. I took a good look at him and he looked so lethargic. Something wasn't right about him but I wasn't a doctor so I couldn't diagnose him.

"Here goes a gown for him to put on. Get him undressed and the Dr. will be in to see him in a moment. I exited the room and I went on to call other patients. After about an hour the Dr. who was on call pulled me to the side and I hated that he did that.

"I need for you to call Child Protective Services for the child in bed 11. His blood came back and he's ingested alcohol. Had she not bought him in when she did he would be dead now. He's four times the legal limit of a adult." My heart begin to race because I knew I had to call the proper authorities. However, I felt like the right thing to do would be to get in touch with Chloe so that she could at least tell the dad. I was going to try and hold off as long as I could. I pulled out my text and called her but there was no answer so I sent her a text.

Chloe: If you can please get in contact with Corleone. His baby momma and their son are in the ER. Somehow the little boy ingested alcohol and they want me to call CPS. It's my job you know that I have to call but I'm holding out as long as I can. Hurry up!!!!!

I quickly put my phone away and prayed that he showed up sooner than later.

ABOUT AN HOUR LATER

"Where the fuck is my son!" I heard a powerful male voice say. I was getting a patient signed in but I quickly stopped what I was doing to rush out front. Corleone, Dom, and Chloe were all standing in front of the reception desk. I watched as security moved in closer.

"Calm down Bro!" Dom said as he grabbed Corleone by the arm.

"Hello Sir. Can I help you with anything." I said as I gave him this look to let him know to go along with it. He was looking confused at me and ready to snap. Dom whispered in his ear and calmed down a little. This nigga had the coldest set of black eyes I had ever seen.

"Excuse me. This is my brother and his son was brought in. His name is Corleone Demonte Jr." Chloe said.

"Oh yes! Right this way. He's in the back with his mother. Follow me Sir." Before we walked a way I made out a quick visiting pass before going through the double doors that led to the back.

"What the fuck is going on with my son? Your ass better not had called them people or it's going be some shit." He gritted through teeth.

"Shut the shit up nigga! I risked losing my job so that you can get your ass down here and get your son. So please cut it out with all them damn threats. Now to answer your question about what's going on with your son. It seems as though he ingested alcohol and it's four times the legal limit for an adult. It's policy for us to call Child Protective Services but I knew who he belonged to when I saw his name. So I hit my girl Chloe up to let you know what was going on. No need for an apology but you can thank me by copping them gray and white 12's in a size seven that drop Saturday. I hate standing in lines." I winked my eye and I showed him the room his son and baby momma was in. I walked away quickly to the bathroom. I had came all in my panties. This nigga was fine as shit. As scared as I was of him I couldn't help but find myself getting smart with his ass. That kept me from lusting over him openly. I know that I wasn't his type just by looking at his baby momma. I could tell he liked them petite bitches, with flat stomachs, and big asses. I don't meet that criteria so I don't stand a chance with him. I would be lying if I said I wasn't crushing though. It all started when I saw him beating that nigga ass for putting his hands on me.

I never had a nigga take up for me the way them Demonte brothers did. Corleone exuded so much power and that made me want him even more with his psycho ass.

******

All of them doubles I had been working had finally caught up to my ass. I was exhausted and felt like my body as about to shut down on my ass. All I needed was a glass of wine, my Kindle, and my bed. I was off for the weekend and I planned on straight chilling back.

"Excuse me Ms. Brooks." I looked behind me and a man in all black called out to me. He looked like the damn FEDS. I sped up the pace in the parking garage trying to get to my damn car. The faster I walked the faster he walked towards me. I reached in my purse and grabbed my Taser. I was about to light his ass up."

"Calm down. I'm not here to hurt you. Please put that damn Taser away. My boss Mr. Demonte would like a word with you." I looked over him and a black Cadillac truck was sitting in the distance. The back window rolled down and Corleone peered out a little so that I could see his face. My heart immediately begin to race and my coochie started to leak. Lord have mercy I don't think I can be around him without staring at him like a creep. I allowed the guy to usher me towards the vehicle. The closer I got the more nervous I became. The man opened the door for me and I slid inside.

"How was your day?" Corleone asked as he stroked his beard. I had to turn my head when he licked his pretty pink lips.

"It was okay."

"I'm over here. It's rude to talk to someone without making eye contact. It shows a sign of weakness. With that mouth you got I know your ass not weak. Now let's try this again. How was your day?" I turned just a little so that I could look him in the eyes.

"It was okay. And yours?"

"Hectic. This is for you. Thank you for looking out for my son." He handed me two big gift bags.

"Oh no! You didn't have to get me anything."

"Your ass better open them gifts. My feet hurt for standing in line for your smart mouth ass." His phone rang and he answered quickly. I saw him gesture to the driver and we pulled out of the parking lot. I looked inside the bag and it was the Mike's I told him to get for me. I looked inside the other bag and pulled out a gray and white Nike windbreaker with stretch pants to match.

"Fuck! Head to the estate Joe." He said and his driver pulled out of the parking lot.

"Wait a minute nigga! Let me out."

"I'm not done thanking you. Sit back and get comfortable. I need to handle some shit real quick. It will take a minute. It's the weekend. Your ass ain't got shit to do. Fuck with a nigga like me." He gently pushed me back in the seat. His cold black eyes were right back and I could tell whatever phone call he had just received was not a good one. I was not about to be arguing with this psycho ass nigga. I just set back and kept my hand in my purse. I had every intention on tasing his ass if he was on that fishy shit. On the upside of all of this I couldn't believe I was actually in this fine ass nigga car. I was so damn nervous I was sitting on my hands to keep from biting on them. Since Corleone was so engrossed in his thoughts. I pulled out my phone and texted Chloe. She had moved in with Dom and I hadn't heard from her ass.

Me: Girl I'm in the car with this crazy ass nigga Corleone.

Chloe: I know. Who do you think told him your work schedule? Lol

Me: I'm kicking your ass bitch. This nigga done kidnapped me. Keep your phone by you just in case I need you to come get me. His ass ain't wrapped too tight.

Chloe: Girl bye. Corleone is cool. He just don't take no shit. Loosen up British. You never know he might be the one to sweep you off your feet.

Me: I doubt it. I'm not his type. I'm a fat girl. He likes them model like bitches.

Chloe: You're beautiful British. Stop calling yourself fat. In my opinion your ass is thicker than a snicker. Relax and call me when you make it home. Just live a little and let him thank you.

Me: Okay. Ttyl

After about an hour of driving we arrived on a deserted road. We pulled up to a massive gate with a huge gold lion head in the middle of it. The driver reached out and rubbed his hands over it.

The gate opened and he drove in. As we drove down the long driveway which was as long as a city block. We finally stopped in front of one of the hugest houses I head ever seen. What tripped me out was that there were about six other houses in close proximity. Then I remembered Chloe telling me about the Demonte compound. My damn friend had hit the jackpot if she was living in this lap of luxury here. My only question was why would he bring me out here. He doesn't even know me like that.

"Stay here. I need to handle some shit in the house. I'll be right out." Corleone quickly hopped out of the and rushed inside with the driver behind him. I don't know why but a funny feeling came over me like something was about to pop off. I was so not in the mood for this shit today. To kill time I logged on to IG to see what the rich, famous, and stupid were up to. A couple of seconds later Corleone walked out carrying his son.

"Give me my son Corleone! Let me go! I promise I'll stop drinking. Please don't take him from me." His driver was holding her back.

"I'm done with your ass. Pack your shit and be gone before I get back. Get that drunk bitch off of my property." Corleone got inside the car and placed his son beside me. As he strapped him the door where I was sitting at flung open and his baby momma stopped in her tracks when she saw me.

"Really Corleone? You fucking fat bitches now! Wait a minute. It was you. You called him when we were at the hospital!" Before I could react this bitch had hauled off and hit me. I quickly got out of the car and commenced to kicking her ass.

"Bitch you got me fucked up!" I yelled as I got that bitch on the ground and start beating her ass.

"Okay that's enough!" I felt myself being lifted off my feet and carried towards the house. At the same time I observed Chloe and Dom rushing up the driveway.

"What the hell is going on?" Chloe asked.

"Get me the fuck out of here! Take me home Chloe." I was yelling and kicking trying to get out of Corleone's arms.

"Man calm your ass down. You ain't going nowhere. I owe you big time and I haven't repaid my debt. Sis Take her and Jr. over to ya'll spot. Let me get this bitch out of here and out of my fucking life." He gave me a stern look and I just rolled my eyes as I walked off with Chloe. This whole scene had me confused. How is it that every time I'm in the presence of this nigga I'm getting punched in my face? This shit is crazy and I want no parts of it.

Chapter 5- Corleone

"So that bitch the reason why you don't love me no more. I can't believe you left me for a fat bitch. This shit is comical." Sasha was standing in the driveway looking fucked up. British had laid hands on her ass and she was still talking shit about the girl.

"You want to know what's comical. Your drunk pussy ass standing here acting like a motherfucker did you wrong. Bitch, this shit is over so face it. I didn't leave you for nobody. As a matter of fact me and that girl don't fuck around but I would rather fuck with a beautiful BBW than a alcoholic ass bitch who drinks all day every motherfucking day. Not to mention a careless ass mother. Did your drunk ass forget you left Vodka unattended and our son drank it? Fuck off my property before I murk ya bitch ass." This bitch had me so hot that I wanted to kill her ass. I never thought a woman I once loved with all my heart could become a bitch I hated with everything within me. I gave Joe a head nod and he knew to get that bitch off of my property. I took off walking towards my brother Dom house. I hated that my son had been exposed to this shit between Sasha and I.

"Please Corleone! Don't do this! I promise I won't drink again. Just give me another chance. I love you. You're all I have in this world. Please! I'm sorry! I'm sorry!" Sasha continued to cry and scream as Joe dragged her ass off the premises. Her ass comes from money so she ain't getting put out on her as without anything. Bitch is a trust fund baby. Hopefully, her parents can get her some fucking help because I'm done with her ass and she will not see our son again until she is clean.

When I walked inside of Dom's house his housekeeper Bonita was bandaging British's fingers. She looked up at me and rolled her eyes.

"Good Evening. Mr. Demonte.

"Hello Bonita. Thank you." I nodded to her letting her know that she was dismissed. Although she was Dom's housekeeper she works for all of us from time to time.

"What the hell going on now? Girl your ass over here starting fights again." My brother Lucci said as he walked into the kitchen where we were.

"I didn't start shit. Take me back to my car nigga. Your crazy ass baby momma made me break my nails and she fucked my fingers up. That bitch lucky I didn't kill her with my bare hands." She hopped off the bar stool and pushed passed me and my brother. We just stood looking at her ass walk away. Her mother should have named her ass big booty Judy cause she had ass for days.

"That girl crazy than a motherfucker!" Lucci said as he laughed. I just stood watching her walk down the long corridor out of the kitchen.

"Call me crazy but I think I'm in love with her thick ass." I had never really chose a bitch I usually got chose. Sasha and I were more so an arrangement between our fathers that grew on both of us. The only good thing that came from that was our son. I hadn't really been in the presence of a woman who paid me no attention.

Women want to fuck with a nigga because I'm rich and my last name. I can tell British gives less than a fuck about who I am. The name Demonte holds no merit in her eyes. That alone makes me attracted to her. I want to know more about Ms. British. I need to know what makes her tick and her pussy wet.

Coming Soon!!!

THE
ST. PIERRE BOYZ
All Is Fair In Love
& War

Written By:

Mz. Lady P

&

Mesha Mesh

Chapter 1- Leilani Brooks

The last week of my life had been a complete and total blur for me. Life as I knew it had changed within the blink of an eye. I can still hear the doctor telling me that they were sorry but he didn't make it out of surgery. Those words crushed my heart and my soul. Knowing that I would never be able to hug, kiss, or make love to June again. That shit was breaking a bitch down mentally that accompanied with other revelations about him.

He had been everything I could ever ask for in a man. He taught me how to live life to the fullest with no worries or no regrets. Unfortunately, my biggest regret would be not telling him how much I loved him before he was shot down like a dog in the streets.

June and I had been together since I was fifteen years old and he was twenty. My mother Dotty ran a brothel on the Eastside of Dallas called Auntie Dot's Place which was originally her mother's spot. It had been passed down over the years.

See selling pussy was hereditary in our family. From a young age I was groomed to fuck a nigga out of every dime he had in his pocket. My mother taught me that there is power in the pussy but your brain and thought process will make a nigga think you have magical powers. Dotty used to say if you can make a nigga come up off that bread simply off conversation then you're a bad bitch. I was a bad bitch without a doubt.

At fifteen I was hitting licks with Dotty and fucking some of the biggest niggas out of Dallas. In reality Dotty was basically pimping me out but I didn't see it like that. Dotty was teaching me how to live and I'm forever grateful for her being my mother. She taught me that life ain't peaches and cream. You have to get out in the world and hustle to get whatever the fuck you want out of life. She instilled in me to never work for another motherfucker. Be your own Boss and stay bossed up on these regular bitches.

Junario "June" Cokes was a hustler that was well known all over Dallas. He was ruthless savage ass nigga that didn't give a fuck. He was all about his bread. That was one of the main reasons Dotty put me on him. He was having a party and wanted some of her girls to service some of his crew. She had me there serving drinks but in reality I was bait. She dangled me in front of his ass like worm on a hook. Just like the fish he was he snatched my prey up quick.

I was all for taking his money but that quickly changed when he got me alone. It was just him and I in the room so I was able to fully focus on him. He was a redbone nigga with these mesmerizing gray eyes. He was tall in stature and rocked a low cut fade. His hands were so soft as he caressed my body. I was asshole naked ready to give him some pussy and get paid so I could get ready for the next trick but June had other plans for me. That night we didn't even fuck he made me get dressed and we talked for the rest of the night.

Unbeknownst to me, after he left he pulled Dotty to the side and paid her ten thousand dollars to have me with the stipulation that I was never to turn a trick again and I was to fuck him and him only. Dotty was not about to let that type of dough pass her up. She took him up on the offer and I had been with June ever since. That was fifteen years ago.

June took me away from the life that I was accustomed to. He showed me a better way of living. With him I finished high school and I graduated from college with a Degree in Nursing. I never had to work or lift a finger. June took great care of me and made sure I wanted for nothing. He just always wanted me to have something to fall back on if shit went left.

I was no longer in the business with Dotty but over the years she became too old to run the business. June helped me to legalize what she had been doing by turning Aunt Dot's into one of the biggest strip clubs in Dallas. With all the damn education I had my ass still ends up being a Madam at what was now my strip club. I was no longer in the business and I made sure shit was legal. I didn't allow my girls to sell pussy on the premises. Do that shit on your own time. My establishment was strictly for entertainment. Any girl that worked for me had to either be in school or working towards a life goal. I wanted to set the bar higher than just popping pussy for a nigga that was throwing money.

June gave me a better outlook and mind frame on life. It was because of his expertise I was richer than what most people thought I was. I thank God for him saving me from what would have probably been detrimental to my life. It's crazy that he gave me a better life and lost his life for the way he lived his. June was still a hustler and was feared by the streets. However, times had changed and new hustlers moved in and ultimately waged a war to take his spots. June wasn't going period. He wasn't about lay down willingly so they laid my baby down permanently. They killed him coming out of the home he shared with his wife and their three children. A family I never even knew existed until I was asked to leave the hospital so his family could mourn in peace. I cried my heart out when I was denied access to see his body one last time. In a matter of minutes the life I thought we had was reduced to nothing. In the eyes of the law and his family I was a nobody. The secret son we shared was a nobody. The same son he said we had to keep a secret so that he would remain safe from the shit he did in the streets was really a secret because he had a family.

******

Exotic cars from all over the world were aligned along the streets as I passed by the church where the love of my life's service was being held. Business men, crooks, politicians, cops, dope boys, and whoever else you can name were all in attendance. Anyone that knew June knew that he was either one or two things; respected or feared by his peers. Some traveled hundreds of miles and took time out of their busy schedules to pay homage to their fallen soldier who had been nothing but solid since their first encounters, and some were there just to make sure he was really dead. With tears cascading down my face, I sadly looked through the rearview mirror at my son, who was an exact replica of June, as he happily played with his seatbelt and sucked his thumb not fully understanding what was going on. As soon as he felt my stare, he lifted his head only to be met with my saddened eyes, and he smiled angelically making me feel a little better. Things were crazy and I didn't know what I was going to do when he asked for his daddy. How am I supposed to look in his face and tell him that there is no daddy to hold mommy at night, no daddy to wipe away his tears, and no daddy to teach him how to be a man? However, I shook those thoughts away; now was not the time to worry about any of that. At that moment all I wanted to do was say my goodbyes and there was nothing anyone could do or say that could stop me from seeing June one last time.

As I looked around to find a good space to park, a vacancy by the front door of the of the church caught my attention so I quickly swooped on in. Before stepping out, I closed my eyes, said a quick prayer, and then fixed the Gucci shades on my face. With all troubles given to God, I stepped out of my vehicle, and then retrieved Junius from the back seat.

"Everyone please stand to view the body and make sure to keep it brief so that his loved ones can have a few extra moments with him before he's laid to rest," the preacher said no sooner than I graciously entered through the double doors.

The choir sang "Stairway to Heaven by the O'Jays as rows and rows of people in all black attire stood off to the sides in the pews waiting for the usher to signal that it was their time to go. Instead of falling in line like everyone else, I continued my strut right on down the center aisle with my head held high and my son's hand wrapped tightly in mine turning heads. The black lace mid length dress hugged my curvaceous body just right and the women pulled their husbands behind them. My hat held a small black veil which only covered a small portion of my face. On that day, I wore a small amount of makeup so I wouldn't run the risk of destroying it with my tears but I was still cute. Stunned by my actions, people pointed in my direction and whispered, while trying to figure out who I am. Her family may didn't know, but majority of his partners did, and they nodded their heads at me in recognition. These bitches can play crazy all they want to, I may not have been his wife but I was that bitch that held him down in more ways than one so she got to respect that. I don't know if she knew about me but I definitely didn't know about her so I held no beef in my heart for her, but I wasn't going to put up with any disrespect if she came at me wrong.

"Aww hell nah, what is this bitch doing here," June's wife screamed and stood from her seat when she noticed it was me who had everyone's attention. "You gotta go now, you are not wanted here."

As if I didn't hear her, I kept going until I made it to his casket. A lone tear escaped my eye, my throat felt like it was closing, my heart rate sped up, and I felt as if the wind had been knocked out of me when I felt his cold cheek. Before that dreadful moment, I knew him being gone was real, but seeing him laid out in his casket seemed to really seal the deal. Mixed emotions ran rampantly; on one hand I was angry at him for how he played me for stupid and didn't keep it real with me. But on the other hand, my heart still wanted who it wanted, which was him.

"Daddy, daddy," my son screamed excitedly as he struggled to break free from me.

Upon hearing him, the crowd gasped, and all hell seem to break loose, but I didn't have time to see what was going on. My focus was on June and my son. I was stuck not knowing what to say or what to do when Junius cried because I wouldn't let him go to his dad. A commotion behind me could be heard, but still, my attention never wavered from June's face. That is, until I felt a strong tug of my hair which caused me to fall backwards, taking my son down with me. No matter how hard I fought to get up, I couldn't. His bitch ass wife had one hell of a grip on my extensions. With punches raining down on my head, I defensively placed my arm over my face to try and shield some of the blows. My son, frightened out of his mind, screamed to the top of his lungs and I reached out to him but was roughly pulled back once again.

To break it up, someone grabbed June's wife from behind and tried to pull her away, but she had a mean grip on my hair. Several people ran over to assist, some even wrestled with her trying to pry her hands away. It took a minute, but as soon as I was able to move it was on. I hit that bitch with a combination of blows, putting her on her ass where she needed to be. She didn't know me like that, but she soon found out that she fucked up. All of my frustrations were being taken out on her unmercifully. Next thing I know, I'm feeling blows coming from everywhere; those bitches were jumping me. I didn't give not one fucks though, while they were beating my ass, I was beating hers. Only way I was stopping was if they knocked me out.

Pow, pow, a gun went off causing all of us to instantly become still.

"Let her go," a deep baritone voice demanded with authority.

Afraid for both me and my son's life, I quickly stood and grabbed him up into my arms ready to hightail it out of there. Embarrassment was written all over my face when he looked into my eyes so I turned my head to break free from his penetrating stare. Alarms went off in my head, I needed to get out of there, but I was completely mesmerized. It was something about the way his eyes seemed to undress me from the inside out, starting with my soul. In my mind, I knew what I was doing was wrong, and he was no good for me, but I was curious to find out who this handsome man was standing before me.

"Luxe you better get this bitch out of here before I kill her," June's wife threatened, bringing me back to the situation at hand.

"Nobody has to get me, I'll leave but you gonna have to see me bitch.

With that being said, I turned around once more and placed a kiss on June's forehead before heading for the exit. As I proceeded to pass the mysterious man he grabbed my arm to stop me. He snapped his fingers, and signaled for one of his goons to walk me to my truck.

"You don't have to do that. I'll be okay."

"I know I don't have to but this is what's happening and that's all to it."

With that being said, he lightly nudged me in the goons direction and proceeded to the front of the church to June. From the corners of my eye I took in all of his chocolate skin wrapped neatly in a Versace suit. His bald head glistened, as his well defined jawline flexed with conviction, covered by his neatly trimmed beard. Now was not the time to be thinking about anything or anyone else so I kept it pushing. One day we shall meet again.

Chapter 2-
Luxe St.Pierre

I stroked my beard in deep thought as I sat nursing a glass of Jameson. I sat in a private area observing the comings and goings at Aunt Dot's Place. This wasn't even my cup of tea but this was actually business. I was never the type of nigga that frequented establishments such as this. Stripper bitches didn't move me. As a matter no bitch that sold pussy for a living moved me. In my opinion they were the bottom of the barrel type bitches and I wanted no parts of them. I like my bitches real ladylike with morals, goals, and dreams. A bitch who sold and popped her pussy for a living couldn't even grace my presence. I liked a bitch that was pure and who could keep up with a nigga of my caliber. At thirty-five years of age I haven't met a bitch yet that could keep up and that's why I'm single with no kids. Not to mention the fact that I have a organization to run in these streets. There's no room in my life for relationships or fatherhood. The streets is all a nigga knows. Now don't get me wrong I enjoy having the company of a beautiful woman. I'm just the type of nigga that likes to fuck and send a bitch on her way. No strings attached.

"It's some bad ass bitches up in here. I should have been blessed this bitch with a real nigga presence." My brother Sebastian said as he grabbed one of the dancers and pulled her on his lap.

"Calm that shit down! We ain't in here for pleasure. This shit is business. Where the fuck is the bitch Black Diamond at?" We were in here trying to catch up with this bitch since we couldn't find her nigga. He owed me well over fifty thousand dollars and he had been dodging me. What he needed to know and understand is that I will never chase anyone who owes me . I just touch everything they love until I bring that ass out. This was the first step to showing this motherfucker I'm not the nigga he wants to play with.

"Here comes that bitch now!" Judah said as he quickly jumped up and headed to snatch her ass up. I knocked back the rest of my drink and stood to my feet. Judah dragged her ass by the hair into our section.

"I swear I don't know where the fuck Shawn at. He ran off with my car and all of my fucking savings. Let my fucking hair go Judah! Why are you doing this? You know I would never lie to you." Black Diamond I cried. I narrowed my eyes because Judah had lied to me when I asked about him fucking this stripper bitch. The look in his eyes told me that him snatching her ass up had more to do with it than my fucking bread.

"Shut the fuck up and wipe your face. I'm not trying to hear none of that shit you spittin right now!" Judah slapped the shit out of her and threw her to the floor. I kneeled down in front of her and lifted her chin so that she could look me into my eyes.

"If I find out you're lying I'm going to feed you to my pit bulls." I spoke through gritted teeth."

"I swear to you Luxe. I'm not lying. That nigga took every fucking thing I owned. Do you actually think I would keep his whereabouts a secret? He fucked over me and I hope and pray you find his bitch ass." She cried and rushed out of the section we were in. I watched as she tried to walk pass my brother. He blocked her and I watched her flinch with each word he spoke. This little nigga was going to make me fuck him up. I swear Judah has been a pain in my ass since he could walk. This nigga had some major shit going on with this girl. I would holla at him later about the shit.

Since I had already handled the business I came for I was ready to bounce but I knew my little brothers weren't. So I ordered me another Jameson and chilled back.

"Would you like a dance Luxe?" A redbone thick chick asked as she approached the section.

"I'm good Lil baby. Your ass is sweating like a Hebrew slave. Take that hot pussy over there and fuck with one of them lame niggas." I shooed her ass away like she was a fly. I pulled out my phone and started checking my emails. I had some business ventures and real estate that I invested in so I liked to always keep up with emails.

"Excuse me but I'm going to have to ask you to leave my establishment. Manhandling my girls and not spending money with them is against the rules. As you can see this is a strip club and we require that you spend that green shit that I know you have in your pocket. Ain't no sightseeing in Aunt Dot's Place." I looked up to see who in the fuck was talking to me. I was taken aback when I realized it was the bitch that June fucked with. At the service I was able to get a good look at her because she was getting her ass whooped. I must say she was a beautiful woman. She was stacked like a Stallion. Nice shaped ass and a rack out of this world. Her light skinned tone and long jet black hair had her looking like a ghetto Pocahontas. She was without a doubt the most beautiful woman I had seen in a long time. I moved my toothpick around in my mouth as I sized her up. She was standing over me with her hand on her hip and fire in her eyes. I could tell she was a feisty one and had no problem with squaring up with a nigga. The only problem was I was the wrong nigga to square up with. I was about to go in on her ass but I decided to take another route.

"You got that Ma. I've been put out of better places. If this what you call an establishment get your weight up. I ain't mad at you tho. Mistresses got get their bread anyway they can. Keep it cute Lil Ma." I winked at her before placing my shades on and walking pass her ass. Leaving her standing there with the shitty look. I could tell she wanted to curse my ass and I know she most likely was in her head but the comment I made about her being a Mistress had her speechless. I wasn't trying to be an asshole I just call it like I see it. See what Leilana Brooks didn't know was I knew exactly who the fuck she was but she had no idea who I was. If she did she never would have come at a nigga the way she did. I could almost guarantee are paths would cross again. I'm the King of the city so she had no other choice but to see me.

Chapter 3
Leilani

Who in the fuck did this nigga think he was? This is the second time he has handled me like I was a lame ass bitch. The comment he made referring to me as a Mistress had a bitch 38 hot. This motherfucker didn't know me or my story so how could he ever pass judgment on me or my life. Tonight was my first night being back at work since June's death and this motherfucker had me wanting to take my ass back home. I was sitting in my office when I looked at the security cameras and seen him and another guy manhandling one of my girls. That shit was out of line. Here I was paying these big ass burly niggas to protect my girls but it was obvious that they feared this nigga whom I now know to be named Luxe. I didn't give a fuck what his name was I wasn't scared of his ass. I hated that he was so fucking cocky because that nigga was even sexier than he was when I first saw him at the funeral. His swag and his style was official. He was rocking Balmain from head to toe. It was a shame that his cockiness overshadowed his sexiness. His bald headed ass was going to miss out on a good ass woman. Not that I'm interested in his ignorant ass. I'm just speaking in general. I walked until I found my head of security named Big Boi. His ass was standing on his post like he was really working. His fat lazy ass wasn't doing shit.

"What's going on Boss Lady?"

"I'm trying to figure out why you and the rest of the security team allowed Diamond to be assaulted by those men. He was sitting in a fucking VIP section not spending no fucking money. I'm lost as to how he was even able to get that booth. Please enlighten me Big. You of all people know how I am about the girls being mistreated. I don't give a fuck if they are strippers. These niggas will respect them while they are in my place of business. Now I'm waiting on an explanation because that nigga slapped fire from Diamond. I've seen you stomp mud holes in niggas so I'm lost as to why these niggas got a pass."

"I'm going to keep it one hundred with you. Them niggas are the St. Pierre Boys Luxe, Judah, and Sebastian. They run all of Dallas now that June out of the picture. I have a family to go home to. I'm not about to lose my life trying to protect Diamond from a nigga she fucking. I'm telling you Boss Lady don't be sizing Luxe up. Luxe ain't shit to play with. He's the nigga that's over everything. Judah and Sebastian are his younger brothers. All they ass are crazy and don't care about dropping bodies with witnesses because they know no one will trick on them. Now I understand if you want to let me go but believe me when I tell you no nigga you hire is going to stand up to them crazy niggas. June tried it and well you know where he at."

I stood listening to Big but the only thing that stood out was what he said about June. I didn't want to jump to conclusions but it sounded like he was saying this nigga had killed my baby. Just thinking about June made my heart ache. I couldn't even respond to him. I just walked away and went back up to my office. I closed my door and grabbed June's phone that I had found in his car that was parked in our driveway. I had been trying my best not to go inside of it because I was too afraid of what might be in it.

I powered it on and placed it on the charger so that I could go through it without it cutting off. I knew the code so I just put it in. The phone opened right up. I bit me bottom lip holding back the tears. His screensaver was of his wife and their two kids. I opened up my laptop and connected his phone to it with a USB cord. All of his pictures came up. Everything was there. It was pictures of them at Disney World, Dominican Republic, South Beach, and whole bunch of other places. I was so fucking jealous looking at his wife. She was so pretty and just by looking at the pictures I knew he loved her and their kids.

It wasn't so much that they were on pictures it was the fact that he always acted as if he hated pictures. It was crazy that I had to sneak and take pictures of him while he slept. This nigga never took a picture with our son. I felt so fucking stupid. All of these years all of the signs of him having a double life was now so evident. The more I thought about the shit the angrier I became. My son had been asking about his father and why the mean lady was fighting me. I felt like shit. I didn't have the heart to tell my son I was fighting his father's wife. Shit was so crazy. The thing that was crazier was the fact that my mother had been dodging me. Although she wasn't in the best of health we still talked daily and I visited weekly. I just didn't understand. As much as she loved June one would think she would at least have wanted to pay her respects but she flat out refused. Here I am her daughter and I'm having a rough time dealing with this shit and she's avoiding me. Now that I think about it everybody was different towards me. His crew acted as if my son or me didn't exist but when June was alive they were always around showing respect. All of this fake shit going on. I don't know who is real or who I can trust.

A knock on my office door brought me out of my thoughts. I quickly closed my computer and got myself together.

"Come in!"

"Do you have a minute?" Black Diamond said as she walked in fully dressed with her work bag. She looked so pitiful at the same time I couldn't feel sorry for her ass until I knew what the hell she was mixed up with.

"Yeah. I was just about to call you in here anyway. What the hell is going on? You know my policy about bringing personal shit to work."

"I know and I'm sorry. They were here looking for my ex Shawn. That nigga owe Luxe a boatload of money and they think I know his whereabouts but I don't. That nigga robbed me blind and disappeared on my ass. I wish I did know where that nigga was at. He better hope I never find out because I'm going to sell his ass out faster than a New York minute. I don't know what I'm going to do because he took everything. That's why I've been coming in every night. I need money for an abortion." I felt so bad for Diamond because she looked so scared and afraid. I stood up from my desk and went around and wrapped my arms around her.

"I'm sorry this is happening to you. Does Shawn know that you're pregnant?"

"I'm not pregnant by Shawn." She said as she wiped the tears rom her eyes.

"Well who is the father Diamond? You need to be getting the money from that nigga."

"I'm pregnant by Luxe's brother Judah but he thinks I'm trying to trap him. I would never do him like that. I love that man Leilani but he's questioning everything because he thinks I knew about Shawn staling their fucking money. Now he's acting like he hates me but at the same time trying to run my life. I don't know what to do. Shit is all bad for me right now."

"Well you know I'm here if you need me. Don't let that nigga put his hands on you like that. That shit is not cool. Take you a couple of days off to figure out what you want to do. You know I can't have you out on the floor pregnant. Do you need me to call you a cab or anything?"

"He's actually outside waiting for me now. Let me go before he start going crazy on me again. I'll text you when I make it home." I sat in awe watching her stupid ass talk about how this nigga wasn't claiming her baby but she looked like she was happy he was outside waiting on her ass. This was the same nigga that I saw slap her ass into the middle of next week. I shook my head as she walked out of the door. In a way I felt sorry and then again I didn't. However, I was in no position to judge anyone on the choices they make. I just hope and pray that everything works out for her.

******

The next morning I woke up to the sound of someone banging on my door. I swear I was about go the fuck off on whoever it was especially if they woke my son up. We both sleep late on the weekends so it was definitely about to be some shit. I didn't even ask who it was or look out of the peephole. I just yanked the door open and I there was a man standing on my doorstep with a clipboard but over his shoulder I noticed my car and June's car being loaded up on a tow truck.

"What the fuck are you doing? Those are my cars." I rushed out and that's when I locked eyes with June's wife standing there with two police officers.

"I'm sorry Ma'am. I'm only doing my job. You've been served." He handed me a manila envelope and I quickly opened it. My heart literally stopped as I read over the contents. I dropped to the ground as I realized what was happening. I had to relinquish all properties that had June's name on it.

"Momma what's going on?" I quickly stood to me feet and rushed over to him.

"Nothing baby but Mommy needs you to go upstairs to your room and pack only a couple of things. Make sure you get your wrestling men. Once I saw that he was back inside the house I walked over towards June's wife. The grin on her face let me know that she was getting a kick out of this.

"Ma'am please step back." The police officer said as I approached.

"Why are doing this you spiteful ass bitch!" I yelled.

"Because I can. This is what happens when you're the Mistress and your married nigga dies with his name being on everything. The wife gets to step in and take all of it. Just to let you know I'm not that petty. You have until the end of the day to be out of my fucking house. You and your bastard son will not be staying in the house that rightfully belongs to me and my children. Now I'm being nice about the situation. Don't be gone off the premises and I will have you arrested. Technically you and your son are squatters." I swear I wanted to beat this bitch ass but the police officer was standing in between us. I swear this bitch was going to have to see me one day with all this disrespect. Yeah I got to get at this bitch for talking shit about my son. I walked away and went back inside the house. As I looked over the paperwork I shook my head in disbelief. June's name was on the lease of my club. That wasn't right. I know for a fact Dottie had the deed transferred over to my name. Something wasn't right.

I quickly ran up the stairs and I tried to pack as much as I could. I knew I wouldn't be able to pack up all of my shit. I cried as I stood looking around at the house I shared with June. This shit was a nightmare. I couldn't believe I was being evicted from my fucking home. A bright idea came in my head as I stood there crying.

"I'm ready Mommy."

"Okay. Remember when I told you to never write on the walls. Well today you can write all over the place. Go get all the markers and pens you can find in Daddy's office. While he was gone I went to the garage and grabbed my steel bat. I just started breaking every window, putting holes in the walls, I broke all of the TV's, I yanked all the cable wires from the walls, I sliced every piece of furniture in the house, and I cut all the water on in the house and stopped it up with rags. If that bitch wanted this house she was going to have to fix the bitch up. I refused to let this bitch think that she was going to move in and live comfortable in the house I had invested so much in.

I called an UBER and headed over to my club but when I made it the doors were chained closed with an eviction notice. There was a side entrance to my office that I had installed that no one else knew about. I placed my key in the door and I went inside. I grabbed my safe and all of my important papers. I placed the safe inside of the UBER and quickly ran back inside. I went towards the kitchen and cut on all of the gas stoves. I grabbed a pair of matches and lit my office on fire. I hurried up and got the fuck out of dodge. I felt no pain as I heard the loud ass explosion in the distance. Did this bitch thing she was fucking with a weak bitch? I would never allow her to have my family's business. Since June fucked me out the life I built. I decided to fuck her out everything she wanted. I quickly headed over to the bank and withdrew the fifty thousand dollars I had in my savings account. Including the twenty I had in my checking. There was no telling what this bitch was going to be up too.

It had been a long day and I just wanted to figure out my next move. Not to mention the fact that my son was tired and I was hungry. I gave the UBER driver five hundred dollars for helping me out all day. He dropped me off at the W downtown. I was embarrassed as hell as the bell boy needed two carts for all of the bags and shit that I had. My ass looked like a damn bag lady.

As if my day couldn't get any worse. I saw the last person on Earth I wanted to see. It was Luxe with some white bitch. I hurried up and put my head down when we made eye contact. He had smirk on his face that hurt my feelings. This nigga was laughing at my struggle. I hurried up and snatched my key card from the Concierge and rushed towards the elevator.

"Leilani!" He roared. I stood frozen because I never remembered telling this motherfucker my name.

Chapter 4

Luxe

Anyone with two working eyes could easily see that something was bothering Leilani by the angered expression she carried on her face. Then when she heard me call her name, she stomped her feet, rolled her eyes in the air, and then snapped her body around making a face that let me know she didn't feel like fucking with me. However, I was curious to know what was going on with her nonetheless. Her tough mask didn't scare me one bit; on the contrary she looked even more beautiful than I had last envisioned. I would be lying if I said I hadn't been thinking about her ever since I saw her that day at the funeral. No matter how hard I tried to get her out my head, I just couldn't. That coupled with the way she checked my ass at the club without so much as an ounce of fear in her eyes, made me more intrigued with her. That bitch had some balls, and I knew it when she walked inside the funeral like she couldn't be fucked with. She didn't give a damn about being outnumbered, or about the consequences of her actions. All she knew was that the nigga she fucked with was being buried, and not a soul could stop her from attending. That's the type of bitch I had to have on my team. When it comes to picking my woman I got to know deep down inside that if shit get tough she can handle whatever comes her way and she won't fold under pressure.

For a moment, I was stuck, and just stood there mesmerized by the mere sight of her. I can't lie, she had my mind gone, and I wasn't paying attention to anyone, or anything else around me. On the cool though, I could see why June snatched her lil ass up.

"Who is she," the irrelevant bitch who was hanging on my arm asked with her face twisted in jealousy as she nudged my side. "So you just gone disrespect me like that?"

"I don't have time for this shit dude, handle whatever it is that you have with this white bitch, and just holler at me some other time," Leilani threw over her shoulder as she walked away.

"Who you calling a bitch, bitch," the snow bunny threw back.

Leilani stopped in her tracks, and then looked down at her son who was holding her hand before turning back around to face us.

"You know what," she grimaced. "I'm going to let you make it because I have my son with me, and you better thank God, because the way I'm feeling right now I could fuck both of y'all up."

That happened fast, and I was so caught up by her beauty that I almost missed it. Coming back to reality, I pushed Snow off of me, and fished in my pocket for a twenty, "Here bitch, go catch a cab. You doing too damn much considering you just a fuck."

"But Luxe, you said we were going to have lunch," she whined as she grabbed the money out my hand.

After snatching the money back, I snarled at her, "I was gonna do that too, but you fucked that up asking me questions. Now hurry up and go before I fuck you up.

If looks could kill, I would have been burned at the stake, but she knew better than to try me. Instead of saying anymore, and running the risk of me breaking her jaw, she just turned around, pointed the fuck you finger at me, and then walked away while cursing me out. Fuck, I said to myself as I ran towards the elevator to catch up with Leilani. Fucking with Snow I almost missed my chance to see what was going on. By the time we were done with our conversation, Leilani had walked off again, and was about to get on, so I quickly rushed over before she could get away. The door was almost closed, but I placed my arm inside, so it could reopen, and then I stepped in.

"I know you heard me call you."

"And I know you see my tired son," she pointed to the little boy holding her hand.

Ignoring her attitude, I kneeled down, and rubbed little man's curly head, "What's up my dude."

"Hi," he said while smiling and waving at me.

I could tell he was a cool little guy just by how he responded, so I reached in my pocket, took out a few bills, and handed them to him. His eyes lit up like the Fourth of July, and he quickly stuffed the bills in his pocket.

"You don't have to do that," Leilani said.

I ignored her once again and stuck my hand out to dap little man up, "Use that to buy yo momma dinner or something, okay. Maybe she'll stop being so grumpy."

"Okay," he dapped me back and placed his hand by my ear so he could whisper. "I hope she like it because she have been kind of fussy," he said and we both laughed at her expense.

Once we were done with our conversation I stood up, and faced a gorgeous, but stressed looking Leilani. Even with her hair wrapped in a scarf, and her house clothes on she was still sexy as fuck.

"What are you doing here with all that stuff," I pointed to the luggage that the bellhop who was pushing. "I know June didn't leave you hanging, or did he?"

"That's none of your damn business. I didn't ask you about the white girl, don't ask me about my life," she replied with much attitude.

"You got a slick ass mouth but I can tame that," I smirked and then licked my lips seeing as how she was watching them so much.

She placed her hand on her hip, "I'm not scared of you like all these niggas around here so you can miss me with that."

"Look, all I was tryna do was maybe offer yo homeless ass some help, but since you wanna be a bitch I'll take my help where it's needed."

"Do that," she sassed.

Her attitude was the truth, and although I didn't play that shit with women, I was turmed on like a motherfucka. She had her back turned to me as I continued to stare in her direction, and all I could visualize was me grabbing her by the face, and shoving my tongue down her throat to hush her big ass mouth. I had my job cut out for me if I really wanted to fuck with her, but I was going to tame that shit. Lil momma was definitely a piece of work, but I'm up for the challenge.

The door dinged, and she stepped into the hall without acknowledging my presence any further, but I was still behind her anyway.

"Didn't you get the cue that you wasn't needed," she asked as she placed her key in the door to unlock it.

"Nah, I didn't, hence the reason I'm still behind you," I replied with a cocky grin on my face.

After she stepped inside, she looked me dead in the eyes, and placed her hand on my chest, "You're not welcome in here so I suggest you turn ya ass back around and leave."

I politely moved her ass out my way, and went to take a seat on the sofa, "You might as well cut the bullshit and come make yourself comfortable."

With her hand on her hip she grimaced, "If you don't get the fuck out I'm calling security."

"Oh yea," I smiled and then turned to the bellhop. "My nigga Drizzle, she said she calling security. Where Tony and Rock at so I can tell them for her."

"They somewhere around here, ain't no telling with those niggas. They do everything but secure this mothafucka," he joked.

"That's what I thought," I turned to Leilani. "You still want to call them?"

She didn't waste anymore time with the extra shit and just stormed away.

"Fuck you, I don't even know yo ass like that but I already hate you nigga," she said loud enough for me to hear, but low enough that her son couldn't.

I laughed right in her face too. Ignoring her ass was beginning to be a ritual, and she seemed to hate that more than anything. Seeing as though she couldn't shake me, she roughly snatched their things off the buggie, and then stomped in the room to get them situated without tipping the bellhop. Since it was my fault she didn't want to give him anything, I tipped him a hundred dollars, and sent him on his way. Almost an hour had passed, and it seemed like she was trying to avoid me by taking forever to get done with what she was doing. Lil June was good company though. Me and that lil nigga hooked up his X-Box, ordered some pizza, and fought hard on Mortal Kombat until our fingers hurt. I gotta say that I loved his competitive spirit, although I was kicking his ass. He didn't want to give up, and neither did I, but when I caught him yawning I let him beat me for the last time so he could feel like he did something.

"Gone take a nap lil man," I instructed him.

He rubbed his eyes, "It's okay, I don't want to leave you in here by yourself."

"Don't worry about that. I'm bout to go get your momma."

"Okay," he said and then laid back on the sofa.

I waited patiently until I heard his light snores and then went to go fetch her ass. She had me fucked up!!!

Coming Soon!!!

Ballad Of A Boss Wife

3

Bless and Bianca's Story

Chapter 1- Bianca

I had been tossing and turning all night. I couldn't sleep for shit in the world. Something was wrong and I could feel it. I had been calling Bless over and over again and there still was no answer. I sat up in bed and went to check on the kids they were sound asleep. I had a bad feeling from the moment Bless walked out the door. I wanted so badly to beg him to send someone else to get Niema and he stay home with the kids of me but that would have been selfish. I know how much he loves his sister and how much she depends on her brother.

I had ben trying my best to stay busy and not think negative but it was just too much shit going on in my life. Finding out Ameerah was my biological mother had fucked me up mentally. All that I could think of was Mina and how she had treated me. To know that she basically kidnapped me at birth had me feeling so down. She put me through so much and only to spite Ameerah and my father. Mina is a different type of evil. I knew in my heart she was a bad person but that bitch is down right sinister. I'm so hurt that I'm numb. Not to mention I feel so stupid. Stupid to the point where I couldn't even reveal to my husband that the bitch had fucked me over in the worst way. I know that my husband will be supportive but I also know that without a doubt he will say that he told me so. I know without a doubt Bless is going to murk Mina's ass when I tell him what the fuck this bitch had did.

I continued to call Bless' phone over and over again. I was still not getting an answer. That made me go into straight panic mode. I decided to roll me a blunt to smoke in the hopes that it would calm my nerves. However, that didn't do shit but make me more paranoid. All types of shit was going through my head.

My doorbell rang and I jumped up and ran to it. When I opened it Sassy and Bolo were standing there. Bolo was holding Sassy up and she was crying. I knew then something bad had happened.

"Man Sis. Get the kids packed we need to head to Chicago." Bolo said sympathetically.

"Is he dead?" I said through tears. Sassy snatched away from Bolo and wrapped her arms around me.

"From the information I got. He was found in the street next to his car with multiple gun shot wounds. He wasn't breathing when he was found. We can't jump to conclusions Sis. We have to get to the Chi immediately. Menace and his girl are going to look over Peanut until Niema makes it here." I heard Bolo talking but I had went deaf after learning that Bless had been shot.

"This shit is so fucked up. He has to be okay." Sassy cried.

Me on the other hand was speechless and in shock. It was to the point where I couldn't cry or scream. I walked away from them and went to the back to wake my kids up. That's when the flood gates started. How am I supposed to tell my kids that there's a possibility their father was dead. I rubbed my hand over my stomach and realized Bless would never get to see this baby. I grabbed Lil Bless and Brianna and held on to them so tight.

"Please God don't do this to me. We need Bless to be okay. There is no way I can go on without him. Please Lord hear my cry and let my husband be okay. I need him more than anything in this world. He's all I have!" I didn't realize I was crying and screaming so loud until my kids were startled and crying as well.

"Come on Bianca. Let's just go. We can grab the kids some stuff in Chicago. I know this is hard but we have to go. The hospital needs you there before they can do anything." Bolo helped me up off the floor and after I gathered myself I prepared to head to Chicago. The entire flight to Chicago I was trying to mentally prepare myself for the news I would learn. At the same time God had bought me this far. There was no way he would leave me now knowing that all I had in this world was Bless.

******

"I thought we were going to the hospital?" I asked Bolo. We were pulling up to a damn house instead of the hospital. I looked on the porch and that's when I saw Bless' friend Blockka. That scared me because he had a serious look on his face.

"We're just following instructions Sis. Come on let's go inside with the kids." I looked at Bolo and rolled my eyes. I was so not in the mood for any of this shit. I needed to know what the fuck was going on with my husband. After getting out of the car Sassy and Bolo grabbed the kids. I walked slowly because I was just too afraid of what I was walking into.

"Aye! Take the kids around back to the guesthouse. My wife Bella and Niema is back there." Blockka said to Sassy and Bolo. Sassy and I locked eyes and I could tell that bitch was just as confused as I was.

"Bloccka pulled me in for hug and gestured for me to walk inside of the house. When I made it inside I almost passed out seeing Bless sitting at the table with his feet up. He was smoking a blunt and sipping some Remy like it wasn't nothing. I looked on the table and saw his bulletproof vest. He must have been wearing it when he was shot at.

"Oh my God! I thought you were dead." I cried as I kissed him all over his face.

"To the streets I am dead. I only sent for you because there was no way I could have you thinking that shit. Plus, I needed to get you and the kids out of harms way. As we speak Trouble and the baby are being airlifted to an undisclosed location until they are healthy. For now I need the streets to believe that I am dead."

"Why?"

"Come here! Let me show you why." Bless roughly grabbed my arm and pulled me down some steps. I covered my nose because the smell had me about to vomit. I could see someone tied to a pull table but not the face. I gripped Bless tighter the closer we got.

"Ish?" He was beaten to a bloody pulp. I was surprised he was still alive

"Yeah that's your little bitch ass boyfriend. What do you know that nigga is Chink little brother. He sent his little brother to handle his weight. Ole bitch ass nigga. See this what will happen when you sniff up behind another nigga pussy."

"Nooo! I can't look at this." I was trying to go back up the stairs but he quickly pulled me back.

"This the same nigga you was Facetime fucking. You had no problem with showing him my pussy so you shouldn't have a problem watching me murk his ass behind it." I watched as bless beat Ish to death with a steel baseball bat. Blood matter and flesh was flying everywhere. The sound of his bones cracking was making me cringe.

"Okay Bless. I get it." I rushed out of the basement and he was right behind me.

"Pull your self together Bianca. I need you get into Boss Wife mode." Bless had grabbed me and pulled me in front of him so that he could look directly in my eyes.

"What do you need?"

"Word on the streets is that Bless checked out. I here the nigga Chinx is celebrating because he think he has the key to the city. From what I hear he's about to take my bitch too. That's exactly what I want him to think. Here's where you come in. I need you to get in and infiltrate his whole operation. If you're scared Bae you don't have to do it. I won't be mad if you don't want to."

"You don't even have to question it. My loyalty is to you. Just knowing that he's behind trying to take you away from me wants me to take everything from him. I'm the wife of a Boss. It's only right I boss up and do what I need to do for my nigga and our family.

"I'm happy you said that. I'd like you to meet somebody."

"Hi I'm Tahari Kenneth. CEO of Boss Lady Inc. and these are the Boss Ladies. We're here to train you for this mission."

Text Shan to 22828 to stay up to date with new

releases, sneak peeks, contest, and more...

Check your spam if you don't receive an email

thanking you for signing up.

Text SPROMANCE to 22828 to stay up to date on new releases, plus get information on contest, sneak peeks, and more!

CPSIA information can be obtained
at www.ICGtesting.com
Printed in the USA
LVOW13s1313270318
571320LV00020B/636/P